Handelman Hill

Jeff Rotter

PAGE PUBLISHING, INC.
New York, NY

First originally published by Page Publishing, Inc. 2018

Cover Art and Author Photo by Amy Hanson – Van Rossum

ISBN 978-1-64214-652-3 (Paperback)
ISBN 978-1-64214-653-0 (Digital)

Printed in the United States of America

For my wife, Fran
Your unconditional love and support mean
the world to me. Love you always!

Chapter 1

As he drove out of town on Highway 70, Paul Handelman opened his driver side window to enjoy the beautiful mid-October afternoon in northern Wisconsin. A fresh rain had fallen in the morning, and the temperature was rising toward an unseasonably warm sixty-five degrees. The leaves on the trees were turning from summer's green into their magnificent oranges, reds, and yellows. To many who lived in this part of the world, autumn was the best of the four seasons, and its wonderful smell filled the air.

About ten miles out of Park Falls, he turned right onto Old Horseshoe Road. Typical of the many secondary roads in the area, it was paved but was in dire need of repair. The long, hard winters had taken their toll, littering the road with an array of potholes and shoulder damage. Paul slowed his Suburban down and weaved through the rough pavement by memory. As the name indicated, Old Horseshoe Road formed a horseshoe shape with only one entrance to the highway. The other end was a cul-de-sac with newer residential developments near the Flambeau Flowage.

Halfway down was a well-maintained driveway framed with oak, maple, and elm trees spaced with precision. Paul entered past the wrought iron gate that had remained in an open state for many years. About two hundred yards in was a fork in the road. On the left, the drive ascended to the top of a hill, which was the main entrance to a gorgeous fourteen-room, two-story estate home. Paul took the fork to the right, which led to the connected three-stall garage. The garage door on the left side was open as he was expected.

The current occupants of the home were Paul's aunts, Rita and Theresa Handelman. They were eighty and seventy-eight years of age respectively and now required assistance to live at home. As the Handelman sisters had the means, there was a group of caregivers that would stop by in the morning and later afternoon to help with cooking, cleaning, and personal care to make sure the ladies were ready for each day. Despite their age, Rita and Theresa remained active and loved visitors as long as it was on their terms. They did not drive anymore but would still go out for lunch or an early dinner several times a week with family or friends.

Paul was the son of Joseph Handelman, Rita and Theresa's younger brother, and had just moved to northern Wisconsin a couple of years earlier from Green Bay. The sisters loved their nephew Paul, and he was "on the schedule" for early Thursday afternoon and later Sunday afternoon. Paul's duties included general maintenance around the house, planning any work that he was not able to do, and most importantly, having a cup of coffee or a beer while visiting with his aunts. In return, Paul enjoyed their company very much, and the twice-weekly visits were a labor of love.

Lately, Paul had noticed that Theresa was developing some fairly serious symptoms of Alzheimer's disease. She would repeat herself often and could not remember recent events very well. When he had asked Rita about this in private during his last visit, a tear had come to her eye as she admitted that the disease was progressing and was starting to cause some hardships. A doctor's visit in early October had confirmed the diagnosis. As the sisters were inseparable, this would be an extremely challenging situation to deal with, and Paul wondered how much longer they could continue living together at home.

The back entrance from the garage led to the kitchen where his aunts would be waiting for him. As Paul entered, he smiled broadly and said in a cheery voice, "Hello, ladies, how are we doing today!"

His aunts' eyes lit up as they smiled.

"Pretty good," said Rita. "Were you going to check the furnace for us today?"

"Yes," said Paul, "but not before I give you both a hug!"

"Oh, Pauly, we love you," said Theresa.

"Well, I am going to get my tools and will be working downstairs on the furnace for a while. When I come back up, we'll have some coffee."

Paul rounded up his toolbox and headed into the basement. A more modern furnace had been installed about ten years ago, but it needed to work hard to heat the large house, so Paul gave it a thorough inspection each year. It appeared the ignitor was a little worn, so he decided to replace it now before it turned into an emergency in the middle of winter. The part would need to be ordered, so the install would have to wait until next week. As Paul replaced the furnace cover, he heard a loud crash from behind the wall.

"Wonder what the hell that was," he muttered to himself.

The noise indicated something had landed hard, so he decided to investigate. There was a room on the other side of the wall from the furnace that was used for storage, so the assumption was something in that space must have fallen off a shelf. Upon entering, Paul noticed that all the stored goods were on the far side of the room away from the furnace and that nothing had hit the floor. There wasn't anything in sight near the wall closest to the furnace either. Inspection from several different angles revealed that it was not one solid wall but probably two. To the casual observer, the plastered wall separating the two rooms appeared to be one and the same, but actually, there looked to be about five feet of space between the walls. It was evident the object had crashed into this hidden area, but how did you enter?

As Paul had been down in the basement for a while, Rita was calling downstairs asking if everything was all right.

"Yes," said Paul. "I will be up in a minute, do you have that coffee ready?" He had also promised his wife, Jill, that they would go out for dinner tonight, so the investigation into the source of this noise would have to wait. Before ascending the stairs, he took a mental inventory of how things looked in the two rooms.

Rita poured and served Paul's coffee. "How is the furnace doing?"

"A part called the ignitor is a little worn, so I will have to pick one up to replace it. Probably next week. We don't want to take a chance of it going out in the middle of winter."

"I agree. Would you be able to come over to take care of some of our leaves also?"

It seems the older people became, the more they worried about things such as the timely raking of leaves, thought Paul. "Of course, I will stop by and clean those up within the next few days."

Theresa had been sitting quietly but all of a sudden asked, "Paul, is everything else good down in the basement? Rita and I don't make it down there anymore as we don't want to fall."

"As far as I know, things are fine." *A rather strange and surprisingly lucid comment from his aunt, considering she was suffering from dementia*, Paul thought. *But who knows what was going through her mind.*

Paul finished his coffee and gave them both a kiss and hug. "Well, ladies, I need to get going as I promised Jill a dinner date tonight. I'll be back soon to take care of the yard work, maybe even tomorrow if the weather is nice enough."

Chapter 2

In the early 1900s, most of Europe was experiencing political unrest along with poor economic conditions, making it very tough for people to survive. Austria was no exception. August and Marie Handelman were struggling like most of their countrymen. August made his living by cutting trees in the forest and selling the logs to local sawmills. On the side, he was an expert woodworker who specialized in ornate wooden furniture that he sold in the local villages. Lately, it seemed, there was not a lot of money coming in from logging or furniture making as even the families that were well off continued to cut back on their spending.

As August and Marie gathered with friends, they heard stories of Austrians who had moved to the new promised land of America. The geography of the upper Midwest portion of America was very similar to Germany and Austria. These tales told of opportunities in farming and forestry as well as a bounty of wildlife. Also, plenty of property was available, some even given to homesteaders for free. It seemed too good to be true, but many were considering a new life away from their homeland.

After some deep contemplation, the Handelmans said their goodbyes and moved to the New World. The journey was long and sometimes grueling but always filled with hope. Eventually, they ended up in northern Wisconsin near Park Falls, which was home to a large population of central and northern European immigrants working in farming, mining, or forestry. The rolling hills and somewhat mountainous terrain of the Gogebic Range reminded them of

Austria, which helped make the transition to their new Wisconsin home easier.

August had the good fortune of meeting a fellow Austrian, John Berger, who ran a local sawmill. John harvested pine and oak logs from the local forests to rough cut boards used in the construction industry. His business was booming, and he needed an experienced forester to help him manage the growth. August was qualified and very interested, so John offered him ten acres of land, help with building his home, and a managing partnership. The B and H Lumber Company became a reality.

Before environmentalism was a movement, August and John were stewards of the earth and believed in replenishing what was taken, which was a way of life for Austrian loggers who had limited land to work with. With the abundance of trees in northern Wisconsin, it was easy to believe that you could just keep clear-cutting forests for decades and never run out. However, this was not the way B and H Lumber did business. Over the years, they purchased forest land with their profits, and other than an occasional clear-cut for farmland, the company replanted on their acreage once the existing trees were harvested.

In July of 1910, Marie gave birth to the couple's one and only child, Robert, who grew up and went to school with a lot of other second-generation American children. In his early teens, he had grown into a tall, strong young man, and as was common in the day, he quit attending school to begin learning the forestry trade by working full-time at B and H Lumber. August's love of the forests and his skills were passed on to his son, who believed firmly in his father's principles. The B and H Lumber Company thrived and persevered through the Great Depression despite the bleak economic times experienced by everyone in the United States. The Handelman family felt very fortunate as they were in a much better place than their family members and friends back in Austria who were still picking up the pieces after World War I.

Even though Robert quit formal schooling early, he knew that learning the English language was the key to success in the United States. Many third- and fourth-generation citizens in the area were well versed in English and rarely spoke their ancestor's tongue. August and Marie continued to communicate mostly in German while their son became fluent in both languages. Robert's language skills proved to be advantageous to B and H Lumber as he was positioned well to establish business contacts including a new venture into finished lumber used in hardwood floors for housing construction. John and August had guided the company well but were not getting any younger. As Robert was respected by his fellow employees and showed great leadership and initiative, the business was sold to him in 1935.

About this time, Robert met his wife-to-be, Greta Werner, at a church social. The daughter of immigrant farmers, Greta also shared an optimistic view of life in America and was fully vested in making the dream work. Greta and Robert soon married and over the next few years brought three children into the world—Rita, Theresa, and Joseph. Robert renamed his company Handelman Wood Products and by 1945 was specializing in finished hardwood flooring and cabinets in addition to the rough-cut lumber. The post-World War II building boom propelled the company to a new level. Their products had a stellar reputation throughout the upper Midwest, and the Handelmans were making a fortune as well as providing excellent employment opportunities to many families. At times, it was mind-boggling to Robert and Greta, but they both used their extensive business skills to make sure the family business continued to prosper.

Among Robert's land purchases was a beautiful tract of property with a large hill overlooking the Flambeau Flowage. As their family was growing and the business was profitable, the Handelmans decided to build their dream home on this parcel. Robert always loved the two-story brick homes, so the fourteen-room estate was erected in 1950. Brownish-gray brick and white wooden framed windows graced the entire exterior while the interior contained a very comfortable, open lower level for dining and socialization. Five bedrooms and a private study comprised the upper level while a large fountain within a roundabout drive fronted the pillared entryway.

While America had rebounded in the 1950s, this area of the country was not wealthy by any means, so the home was the talk of the town. When viewed from the river or Old Horseshoe Road, it was truly majestic and awe-inspiring. The estate was referred to locally as "the mansion on the hill," but after a year or two, this description shortened, and it became known by the name that everyone still uses today, Handelman Hill.

Chapter 3

On the ride home, Paul kept thinking about the noise in the basement, and it was prominently on his mind as he pulled back into his driveway about 5:30 p.m. He was running a little late for his date. His wife was ready and waiting, but it was no problem. Having been married thirty years, not only were Paul and Jill husband and wife, but were also best friends.

"How are the ladies?" asked Jill.

"Doing all right," said Paul. "Sorry I am running late. I'll quick change clothes, and we can go. You look beautiful this evening as usual."

Jill was in her early fifties, very attractive, and could easily pass for a much younger lady.

Paul went upstairs and threw on a fresh pair of jeans along with a new navy blue polo shirt. This style constituted dressing up for dinner in this part of the world—very casual with no pretenses, which reflected the easygoing, friendly nature of northern Wisconsinites. A glance in the mirror revealed a distinguished-looking gentleman closer to sixty years of age than fifty with a full head of hair that was partially gray matching his goatee. It also showed a man who was relatively physically fit but carried the extra twenty to thirty pounds that most Wisconsin middle-aged men dealt with as a result of decades of winters that were just a little too long, food that was a little too good, and a profound love of beer.

"You look nice too." Jill smiled as Paul descended the stairs. "I could go for a good steak. Let's drive out to Club 182."

"Sounds great," answered Paul. "A drink and a piece of the medium-rare prime rib would hit the spot."

Club 182 was about a twenty-minute drive, and as they traveled, Paul was unusually quiet.

"A penny for your thoughts," said Jill.

Paul took a deep breath and began. "Theresa's Alzheimer's is advancing very rapidly. I'm not sure how much longer they can stay in the home. It will come to a point where it will be dangerous for Theresa with the river and the woods. Her short-term memory is almost nonexistent, but she remembers things from the past with no trouble. And today she said something very clear. What a terrible disease, probably worse for the family than for the person who has it. For her part, Rita is handling it well, but I believe she knows they are at the crossroads."

"That seems to be progressing fast. She appeared to be doing pretty good this summer."

"Yes, they just received the confirmed diagnosis from the doctor, and it is moving fast. They have lived on the Hill their whole lives. I can't imagine the reaction if we ask them to move. I suppose we could look at around-the-clock care, but it is costly, and I don't know if we can find that many people we can trust."

Over the next hill, the parking lot of their destination was on the right.

Club 182 was a throwback. The family-run supper club was named after the road it resided on and had a large bar along with some cocktail tables for socializing. No televisions were in sight. Even in 2016, most people put their phones away and engaged in face-to-face conversation without distractions. The bar mixed an excellent Old Fashioned, an extremely popular Midwest concoction served over ice consisting of whiskey or brandy, blended with sugar, bitters, and a cherry which was muddled. Finally, the drink was topped off with sweet, seltzer, or "press," which was half sweet and half seltzer, then garnished with cherries or olives. It tasted like heaven. Club 182 also served excellent steaks, prime rib, and local freshwater fish.

Paul and Jill greeted Jay, the bartender, by name. As he saw them enter, he mixed Jill a whiskey Old Fashioned sweet and waited for Paul. Sometimes it was beer, sometimes not. Tonight it was not. Paul ordered a Glenmorangie 15 single malt scotch on the rocks.

"Special occasion?" asked Jay.

Paul responded, "Not really, just thinking about some bad news. Over the last week or so, we found out one of my aunts who lives on the Hill has Alzheimer's disease, and it is getting worse. So I believe we may be faced with some tough decisions soon."

"Sorry to hear, that's a hell of a thing to deal with." Jay then ambled off to mix drinks for other patrons who were waiting.

Paul again became silent while stirring his drink to let it blend a little in the ice. Knowing him like the back of her hand, Jill looked him in the eye and asked, "Is there anything else that you would like to talk about?"

Paul took a sip of his scotch and began again. "You know me all too well. While I was replacing the furnace cover, there was a crash behind the wall of the furnace room that was loud enough to get my attention. I know they stored a bunch of junk in that back room, but the noise was so loud I thought I better check it out. When I walked in the back room, everything was stacked neatly on shelves on the far side. By the wall near the furnace, there was nothing! I began looking in both areas a little closer, and it became evident that there was about a five-foot space between the walls in the two rooms, and that was where the noise came from! I poked around a little, but then Rita called me upstairs."

"Well, you know the rumors that fly around about Handelman Hill," teased Jill. "Money buried all over the property according to the locals."

"I have to go over there a few times over the next week to rake leaves and fix the furnace, so I'll snoop around a little without them knowing. It sure was strange though. Maybe the rumors are true." Paul laughed and gave his wife a big hug.

Their table was ready, and the couple enjoyed another excellent Club 182 meal. Both of them were very satisfied when they started the drive home, and Paul's burdens seemed to lift. An old Ricky Van Shelton song was playing on the Sirius XM Prime Country station, and he began to sing along: "I need a place where I can lay my head, soft woman and a warm bed, a little time off before I'm dead, I am a simple man."

Jill smiled. *Simple? Far from it*, she thought, but was glad to see him back to himself. *Drinks and dinner with your favorite person in the world almost always make you feel better.*

Chapter 4

Robert Handelman dreamed that his three children would assume control of Handelman Wood Products as he did from his father. Early on, he introduced his love of forestry management to the children. Many happy days were filled with hikes through the northern Wisconsin woods identifying species of trees as well as other plants, birds, and wild animals. He would explain in great detail how the mighty trees were renewable and how the company replanted after harvesting. Once the children were high school age, Robert and Greta initiated them into the business. The girls joined Greta in the office learning to keep meticulous accounting records of all transactions. Joseph, known simply as Joe, worked alongside his father, observing and participating in all the manufacturing and raw material operations.

Rita and Theresa showed great interest in the financial and accounting end of the family business, and both graduated with business administration degrees from the University of Minnesota. Although the lure of the big city with all its glitz and glamour was tempting, their heart and soul were home with their family. The sisters both returned to the Park Falls area and resumed successful careers managing the business operations of Handelman Wood Products.

Joe was very talented mechanically and even at a young age could fix just about any engine or machine that broke down. However, he was fascinated with the automobile, which was becoming the most popular machine in America during the 1950s. Every spare minute, Joe would make his way into Park Falls and visit his buddy George Larsen at his father's car dealership. The boys would talk for hours about the latest engines, and he would help George with any repairs he happened to be working on, learning along the way.

Robert had plans for Joe to follow in his sisters' footsteps and attend the University of Minnesota for mechanical engineering. Upon graduation, he would return and resume his spot in the family business. His son had other ideas. While Rita and Theresa loved every aspect of Handelman Wood Products, Joe was more passionate about automobiles than he was about lumber. As he entered his senior year in high school, talk of college began, and the classic rift began to develop between father and son, the basis of which was the difference in their views of the son's future. Robert respected Joe's love of automobiles but still could not understand how he could throw away the opportunity to one day run the operations of the family business. Despite Robert's misgivings, Joe began working full-time as an automobile mechanic at Larsen Chevrolet in Park Falls after graduating from high school.

Small-town rumors and innuendo began to haunt Joe each day. He was tired of hearing how he had thrown away a fortune, been disowned by his family, and many other proclamations that simply were not true. Joe needed a change of scenery and was open to moving away from the area as long as he could work as a mechanic. His father, now knowing Joe was serious about being an auto mechanic, reached out to his son's boss John Larsen, who was also a good friend. The two of them made a few connections with people they knew, which led to an opportunity for Joe to work at Broadway Chevrolet in Green Bay.

Joe quickly established an excellent reputation as a top-notch mechanic in Green Bay. He saved his money along the way, and when the opportunity to purchase a gas station/auto repair center presented itself, Joe took over ownership of Downtown Auto. During this time, he also met the love of his life, Elizabeth Sumter, and wed her in July of 1958. Joe and Liz settled in Green Bay, and their lives were soon blessed with a son, Paul. A couple of years later, their daughter Catherine entered into the world. Paul loved the automobile repair business just as much as his father and joined him as a partner and owner of three family-run facilities in the Green Bay area.

After arriving home from their dinner date, Paul and Jill decided to have a nightcap out on the deck as the outside temperature was still quite warm and began reminiscing about their early years.

Paul smiled. "Do you remember how we met oh so long ago?"

"Oh, most certainly! I kept passing by the shop on Walnut and Madison Street each night. This great-looking young man was working on an even better-looking '71 Mustang. Finally, I just needed to stop in, at least to see the car." Jill smiled.

"After admiring the Mustang, the young man also caught your eye?"

"Yes, he did. He bought me a Coca-Cola, told me all about the car, and the next day we took a long cruise along the beautiful shores of Lake Michigan. And as they say, the rest is history."

The automobile repair business changed fast in the 2000s and to keep up required a commitment of capital and some very experienced mechanics. As Paul analyzed his financial statements each year, it became apparent the profits were not there like they used to be, and good technicians were hard to find. However, the business had an excellent reputation and was still successful. Although Paul was only in his early fifties, he and Jill decided it was a good time to sell and were able to do so in 2012 for a very nice price. The money received would keep them comfortable the rest of their lives.

Paul and Jill raised two beautiful daughters, Anna and Nicole, who were now living in Chicago and Minneapolis, respectively. With the children gone and no business to attend to, a sort of restlessness set in on the couple as they passed their time in Green Bay. Their finances were such that they could do just about anything. The one thing Paul enjoyed as a child and into adulthood were his visits up north to see his family. He loved spending time with his grandparents and reveling in the wilderness of northern Wisconsin. He continued these journeys north long after his parents had passed away and would visit his aunts and other relatives. Over the years, Paul and Jill had made many friends during their visits, and after some heavy soul-searching, the pull of Paul's ancestral roots won out, and they decided to make Park Falls their new home in 2014.

"You know," began Paul, "I still remember the first few times we visited Handelman Hill to see my grandparents. My father was always a bit apprehensive, but Grandpa and Grandma always made all of us feel welcome. Grandpa would take us all over the woods and waters. Dad never talked much about his parents or the family business, choosing to concentrate on his own business and family instead. Thinking back on the reactions now, I believe my grandfather was proud of Dad but was also disappointed that he didn't stick with the family business. Dad was caught in a tight spot."

"That's kind of what I noticed as someone not part of the immediate family. I could see the compassion and love in your grandmother's eyes when your dad would hug her. I could also feel something was not quite right between your father and grandfather. I'll tell you what though, your dad is one of the finest human beings to have lived, so it hurts me a little to think he had to go through this."

"Dad and Mom had a great life. Not as long as they or we would have liked, but they made the most of it. I couldn't have asked for better parents or a better friend than my father. God, I miss him and Mom too."

Paul's parents had died relatively young, Joe at sixty-four from a heart attack and Liz a few years later at age sixty-six of cancer. The fact that they were no longer around made Paul appreciate each new day even more than he did before. At this moment, his main charge was taking care of his aunts, and the road ahead looked like it could be difficult.

Chapter 5

F riday morning dawned bright, sunny, and warm, promising to be every bit as gorgeous as the previous day. Rita and Theresa were drinking coffee in the dining room, waiting as one of their favorite caregivers, Lisa Morris, prepared breakfast. The sisters now preferred pastries and rolls for breakfast more than traditional choices such as eggs and bacon. Lisa had some cinnamon rolls in the oven this morning, and they smelled delicious.

Theresa seemed to be full of questions today. "Is Paul coming for the furnace?"

Rita replied, "He stopped by yesterday and may be by today to clean up the leaves in the yard."

"I don't remember him being here."

Rita sugarcoated a little. "He was only in and out yesterday."

It appeared that this was going to be a challenging day with her sister.

"We need to take care of our will and finances soon."

"That has already been taken care of, Theresa. We met with Lindsey last month and will finalize everything soon."

Silence ensued as Theresa tried to gather her thoughts. Rita remembered how coherently she responded and asked questions yesterday, only to forget about them today. Thank God they had help. Lisa, with near perfect timing, entered the room with the iced cinnamon rolls.

After breakfast, the questions continued.

"What did Dad ever do with all that land he bought in the Gogebic Range?"

How does she remember this and nothing from yesterday? Rita responded patiently, "He sold the property to a company from Minneapolis. I think they were interested in mining."

"Whatever happened to the money?"

"Some of the money is in the bank, some of it is downstairs."

"What are we going to do with this money?"

"We are not sure. We will talk about that at another time."

As his wealth accumulated, Robert Handelman purchased land at an obsessive pace. At one point, he bought ten thousand acres in the Gogebic Range for twenty dollars per acre. The steep, jagged terrain made this land impossible to farm and very challenging to harvest trees. He was more interested in the possibility of mining and of course making more money. Some local miners were discovering deposits of copper and gold in this region, and Robert was not about to miss out on this action.

At this point, the telephone rang, and Rita picked up as she was near.

"Hello," she said cheerily.

"Hi, Aunt Rita, this is Paul. Just thought I would call and let you know I'll be over this morning to do some yard work. Can you leave the garage open?"

Paul always called before stopping over so that he wouldn't scare them when he came over and to make sure there were no other visitors on the schedule.

"Sure, I'll open it up for you."

"Anyone else coming over today?"

"Lisa is here now, and then Jen will come over to make dinner around five or so, but that is it."

"Okay, we'll see you soon."

The lawn of the estate was expansive, but a large riding lawnmower with a leaf bagger made the job manageable. Paul spent a couple of hours cleaning the yard then stuck his head in through the kitchen door.

"I need to run downstairs again to double-check the part number on the furnace ignitor so I can order it today. I'll be back up in fifteen minutes or so."

He grabbed his toolbox and made his way downstairs. The clock was ticking, and Paul had some investigation to complete.

He started in the furnace room, went to the outside walls and then to the storage room, looking for any way possible to enter the hidden space. Directly behind the furnace was a section of the wall about five feet high and three feet wide that somewhat resembled a door if you looked hard enough. Paul had missed this the first time. He pushed on the left side, then the right. There seemed to be a little movement, but it wasn't opening. There was not a door handle, so a small hook tool was slipped under the left side and pulled. The section of the wall swung open effortlessly, showing magnetic strips framing the inside of the door holding it shut.

He pulled out his flashlight to look around.

"Holy shit!" Paul said to himself. "Unbelievable!"

The light revealed a small hard-sided suitcase that had apparently fallen off the top of a stack of seven more and had opened on contact. Lying on the floor and in the half-open suitcase were stacks of one hundred dollar bills. As he moved the light around, it was clear these were the only objects in the small space, which was about six feet deep.

Paul took a couple of deep breaths to compose himself and did some quick calculations, but his time was running out, so he took a few pictures with his smartphone and carefully closed the door back up. A million questions were running through his head, and he was a little shaken, so there would be no visit with his aunts today.

"Ladies, I have the number of the ignitor, and I need to get back to town to order it. I will be over again on Sunday night to set the garbage and recyclable items out for pickup. Call me if you need anything in the meantime. I love you both."

As Paul maneuvered his Suburban onto Old Horseshoe Road, he began to mildly hyperventilate as he thought about the contents of the hidden room. Where did this money come from? Who else knew about it? Did his aunts or anyone else even know about it? He wasn't sure. Paul did not know Robert Handelman well enough to discern if he was that secretive. Paul's grandmother had passed away at a relatively early age, and his grandfather remained at the estate home with

Rita and Theresa for some years. Outside of his occasional visits, Paul was unsure how many people outside of the immediate family, if any, knew what was actually going on up on Handelman Hill.

Paul needed to learn more about his grandfather's life, and he knew just where to go. He took a couple of deep breaths, picked up his cell, and called his wife. After the voice mail tone, he responded, "Jill, I need to stop and chat with Tony. I'll be home a little later this afternoon. Love you."

Chapter 6

About 1:30 p.m. Paul turned left off Main Street in Park Falls onto Third Avenue. Two blocks down on the corner was an older two-story brick-fronted building with a large Pabst Blue Ribbon sign that stated simply "Tony's Bar." The entrance was graced on the left with a large oval window facing Third Avenue containing a neon Open sign, which was lit up. As Paul entered the nearly empty barroom, a large voice boomed from the far end and started the traditional greeting.

"Pauly, you old horse's ass, what brings you in today, my friend."

"Takes one to know one, you no good son of a bitch, how about a pint of Miller Lite."

Tony Stenson brought the frosted mug over to Paul with a big grin, and they gave each other a hug. Tony was a mountain of a man and a local legend. In high school, he had been a star football player for Park Falls and played two seasons for the Wisconsin Badgers as an offensive tackle before a severely damaged knee ended his career. He returned to his hometown to open a tavern that he still operates today. Tony had been married twice, but the drinking and other aspects of the bar life had taken their toll. In his late fifties, he was single and relatively content with his life as a tavern owner.

Paul found Tony to be very friendly and a good conversationalist, so when the air became too thick at Handelman Hill, he would drive over to see his friend. Tony was also a great source of local history and gossip if you could separate the bullshit from the truth. Always entertaining, just the same.

Paul took a long draw off his mug. "Tony, what can you tell me about my grandfather, Robert."

Tony was not one to mince words.

"What would you like to know? He was a nice enough guy but a little arrogant according to some. Also, he valued his privacy for sure, especially after your grandmother died."

"Did he stay isolated at Handelman Hill all the time?"

"Between there and the business, until he sold that, yes. He spent a lot of time at home."

"Tell me some of the rumors or stories you have heard over the years."

"Why the sudden interest, Pauly? Is something going on with your aunts?"

"You might say that."

Tony was never one to shy away from an opportunity to tell stories to anyone, and this was one of his favorite subjects. "Not sure how much you know, Pauly. Your grandparents did a great job establishing their business and, as you know, became very wealthy. Robert was an excellent businessman and over the years employed a lot of people from the area. But as time moved on and the money accumulated, he seemed to become greedy. The folks in town stated the charitable giving that your grandfather supported over the years stopped. He spent a lot of time at home. Then when your grandmother died, it seemed to get worse. Are you all right if I keep talking about this? I don't know if you want to hear more or not."

Paul took a drink of his beer and nodded, so Tony continued.

"I have to tell you, Pauly. It was just weird that your aunts lived the whole time with their father. The house was big enough, but it was strange that they were never married. Your aunts were committed to the business and were seen around town quite a bit. Rita and Theresa were friendly to everyone, but as time passed, they began to act as their father, seemingly too good to mingle with the common folk so to speak. Nobody knew what was going on up there. They lived a very secretive life for a number of years. Remember, this is just what I and others observed.

"Rumor has it that your grandfather struck gold while doing some test drilling on his Gogebic Range property. He had purchased ten thousand acres of very rough terrain. Paid $200,000 for it. I think he started to get a little bored with the lumber business and this was a welcome diversion. A firm was hired to test drill for copper or other metals and, according to my sources, unexpectedly hit a motherlode of gold in one section. This discovery spurred his interest, and he started to look at the possibility of mining. As you know, the federal and state regulations make it damn near impossible to open up any productive mine and make money. Your grandfather probably spent a good sum of money and time with this, and I think he became very disheartened. The land was eventually sold for $250,000, according to public record, to a company based in Minneapolis in 1988. That was the end of your grandfather's mining adventure."

Paul pushed his empty mug toward Tony, who grabbed it and refilled.

"Interesting story, thanks for sharing, Tony. I don't know too much about my grandfather, but it doesn't seem like him to back away. All those years we visited, he never mentioned the mining, although he did show us the Gogebic Range property. Do you know anything about the company that bought it? Did they ever mine the land?"

Tony answered.

"They tried a few times but kept running into opposition. Once they got by the government regulation, it was constant environmental protests. I believe the company owns it even after all these years but hasn't broken ground yet. The land didn't cost a lot of money, so they are probably waiting for the right political and economic climate. We could use the jobs up here, but passion runs deep for land preservation also. The northern Wisconsin conundrum. Do we take jobs or protect the environment? Always a battle up here, and it seems we can never have both. After that, your grandfather was rarely seen in public. He became very sheltered and, as you know, passed away in 1991."

Paul replied, "Yes, he was eighty years old, a ripe old age for our family. When I think back, there were some changes in his attitude and demeanor, but I chalked it up to old age. Maybe the inability to open up a mine wore away at him as you said. He didn't fail at very many things in his life and always expected to come out on top, which was one of the reasons he was successful with his business. Very intriguing."

Tony asked, "Paul, you mentioned something going on at Handelman Hill. Care to share?"

"Well, Theresa has advanced Alzheimer's disease, and my aunts are struggling a bit, so we're not sure what we are going to do. We have that weighing on us and will have to make some tough decisions soon."

Tony raised his eyebrows and gave him the "come on now, you can tell me" look as he knew there was more to the story. Today Paul wasn't biting though and didn't mention the money. He finished the last of his beer and bid Tony goodbye.

Chapter 7

A newer-model Mercedes Benz pulled into the First National Bank parking lot just before 4:30 p.m. Lindsey Barrington exited with her briefcase and marched into the bank, not bothering to announce herself to the tellers. She had an appointment with her good friend, Vice President Sheila Nackers. Lindsey closed the door behind her, looked Sheila straight in the eye, and said, "It is time."

Lindsey is one of the few attorneys in Price County and by all accounts was very good at her profession. Her claim to fame was defending Johnny Clarkson, who had walked in on his wife and neighbor in bed and made sure it was not going to happen again. Johnny did everything but confess, and the evidence was overwhelming. However, the small-town crime investigation techniques were shoddy. Lindsey mounted a case based on contaminated evidence and presented a lengthy diatribe that confused the jury just enough to cause a mistrial, which ultimately released Johnny from a double murder charge.

Except for Johnny's family and perhaps the neighbor's wife, this was not a popular decision in Price County, but Lindsey didn't care. This court victory just boosted her large ego further. She was an attractive brunette, somewhat wealthy, and in love...with herself. Legal professionals are opportunists by trade, and Lindsey was no exception. It was no secret that the Handelmans had money, and as time passed, the family grew more paranoid and sought legal advice. She offered her services to the Handelmans many years ago and remains Rita and Theresa's legal counsel to this day.

Sheila Nackers forged her career as a banker in the 1980s and now found herself in the vice president's seat. The Handelmans had banked at First National practically since its inception, and Sheila got to know the family members well over the years. They trusted each other, and their relationship continues today. Sheila handles herself well and is well respected in the community.

Both of these ladies had a front row seat for decades into the financial and legal world of Robert Handelman and his family. An interesting world indeed. The amount of money was staggering for this part of the country. Once Robert passed away, the two ladies became very close friends with Rita and Theresa. Every month a meeting would be held to discuss financial and legal matters. As the four enjoyed each other's company, dinner was included in these meetings when the sisters felt up to it, and the time spent together made them almost family in more ways than one.

During the last few visits, it was becoming apparent that Theresa was slipping mentally. Also, Paul Handelman had moved to the area and was becoming a bigger part of his aunt's lives. Time was pressing as nobody knew what would happen legally or financially if one of the ladies fell ill or died, so Lindsey began digging a little deeper into the sister's legal documents. The paperwork involving the sale of the Gogebic Range property seemed strange. She had found the test drill results and wondered why Robert let this land go so cheaply when he knew there was gold there. It didn't make sense. One day she ran across a handwritten paper that stated simply, "$4 million received – GR property." There was no way this money had found its way into the banking system in this area, but where was it?

Lindsay opened her briefcase and showed Sheila the note.

"It is time to ask the ladies what's up with the four million dollars. Where is this money, and who gets it? They were very tight with their father, and I guarantee you that they would know something. There is no mention of this in the will."

"I don't know, Lindsey," Sheila stated. "We are already in their will, and that is worth enough in my mind. Are you sure this is real and worth pursuing?"

As her greed flowed out, Lindsay became animated. "Are you fucking kidding me? It's four million dollars! If I could get a quarter of that, you wouldn't see me in this shithole of a town anymore! It's a ton of money. We need to get everything finalized and sewn up. Their nephew Paul has been hanging around a lot over the last couple of years, and we don't need him jeopardizing anything. We were there for Rita and Theresa when no one else was. We deserve this!"

Sheila didn't know if they deserved anything as they were paid well for their services over the years but knew better than to argue with her attorney-friend, especially when she was raging. "We can bring that up to them when we visit tomorrow, probably after lunch. We will tell them we want to make sure it is in a safe place."

Lindsey got up to leave. "Yes, I need to bring these papers over to their house and put them back in the safe anyway. I'll pick you up around eleven. See you then."

Sheila shut her office door, sat back down, and put her head in her hands. Where was this going to go? She was comfortable with her life and loved working with the ladies. Sheila considered them friends and knew the sisters appreciated the help as finances worried them more and more the older they became. Lindsey had a different point of view and was dancing on the edge of being out of control. Now with the possible addition of four million dollars in cash, she couldn't even imagine what would happen. Tomorrow would be interesting.

Chapter 8

When Paul arrived home, Jill was still out and about, so he immediately logged into his computer to do some research. The first stop was the county land records. His grandfather had sold the property for $250,000 just as Tony had stated. The buyer was Minnesota Resources LLC. Google revealed that the company was in the business of buying land for mining, which was no surprise. The principals were locals from Minneapolis but included more than one person of Chinese descent. As Paul peeled off more layers, it looked like a compelling possibility that Minnesota Resources LLC could be a front company for the Chinese government. Not a surprise either the way the world was in 2016. So in effect, the Chinese government had purchased his grandfather's land in the Gogebic Range. He wondered if the United States government knew or even cared.

Paul decided that was enough for today and grabbed a beer from the refrigerator before walking to the back deck to enjoy the last bit of sunshine on this beautiful autumn afternoon. He tried to wrap his mind around the day's findings, but it was almost overwhelming. Jill pulled in around 6:00 p.m. with a couple of plates of fresh pan-fried walleye she had picked up to find about six empty beer bottles and a full one in Paul's hand.

Jill responded half angrily, "Oh my, you couldn't wait for me to get home before starting?"

"Sorry, dear," Paul slowly slurred. "There were a lot of discoveries today."

Jill replied, "Are you sober enough to tell me about them, or do we need to wait for another time? Please eat something anyway."

Paul wolfed down his walleye plate and waited for Jill. She poured a glass of wine, and they retreated to the family room. Paul pulled out his phone and loudly proclaimed, "Look at this, look at all that money. Where the hell did this come from? Who knows about it? It's driving me fricking crazy!"

Jill's eyebrows raised, and the questions began forming. "Is this from the hidden room you were looking for?"

"Yes! I found it and was able to open the door this afternoon, right behind the fucking furnace!"

"Paul, easy!"

"Sorry, it was right behind the furnace. I pushed, and it didn't budge. Then I slipped a hook tool under and pulled. The door quickly popped open, and there lay the open suitcase on the floor, which apparently had caused the noise I heard. It must have fallen off the pile of the other seven! Those were the only things in the room, and there was not another entrance, at least that I could see. These are stacks of one-hundred-dollar bills, probably five thousand dollars in each stack! I didn't count, but if there are one hundred stacks in each suitcase, that would be four million dollars total!"

Jill was stunned. "I don't even know what to say. Is that the reason you went to see Tony today?"

Paul replied, "I did not know my grandfather that well and needed to find out more after I found the money, so yes, I went to hear what Tony could tell me. It seemed he turned into a recluse after Grandma died. Tony also stated that in later life Grandpa was obsessed with the Gogebic property and allegedly discovered gold during a test drill. He ran into obstacles when trying to mine so ended up selling it for $50,000 more than the purchase price. Obviously, I didn't tell Tony about the cash discovery."

Jill sighed. "Wow. How do you piece all that together?"

"Hell, if I know." Paul shrugged. "It's information overload. I knew nothing a day ago, now today, there is a pile of mystery money. I also researched, and Tony was telling the truth. The Gogebic Range land sold for $250,000 according to the county records. There is some interesting stuff on the Internet though. It appears the company that bought it may be a front company for the Chinese government."

Jill asked, "Seriously? Chinese government? Are you sure the beer didn't affect your research? That seems like a stretch."

Paul got a little perturbed. "Jill, I know I've been drinking, but I know what I've seen. When I did the research, I had just finished two beers with Tony—that was it! There are some threads here that suggest Chinese government involvement. I'm not sure if this makes a difference or if the money is connected, but it seemed weird. I am struggling with how to proceed. Do my aunts even know about this? If they did, why didn't they tell anyone or does someone else know? Do I need to do more research? Before I knew it, I was a six-pack in at home while I was contemplating the events of the day!"

Jill gave him an understanding look. "What a day, and I know you didn't ask for all this. It may be difficult, but try to relax a bit and get a decent night's sleep. We can discuss this in the morning."

Paul kicked back on the recliner and was snoring after about fifteen minutes of watching television. Jill was now wide awake and wondered how many glasses of wine she would need to close her eyes tonight.

Chapter 9

On Saturday morning, Lindsey Barrington slowly opened one eye and caught bright sunshine slipping through the cracks of her bedroom window curtains. She quickly closed her eye and held her head, which was pounding with the hangover they were saving for Judas. Since this wasn't going away on its own anytime soon, Lindsey rose out of bed, put on a robe, and marched into the kitchen in search of pain relief. On her way, she noticed her good friend, Assistant DA Danny Jackson, sleeping on her couch in the living room. Lindsey figured she must have called him for a ride home when driving was no longer an option. Her popularity with the police forces in the area was not favorable, so there was no chance she could ever receive a break if pulled over.

Her memory of the events from the night before was as foggy as her head. She remembered going to Park Falls Country Club for dinner with her friends, then over to Clancy's Lounge on the outskirts of town. Clancy's was about as upscale as you could get in this part of the world, though also attracting young to middle-aged folks of all backgrounds as the drinks were good and the atmosphere was relaxing. Lindsey would need Danny to fill in the blanks. But judging by the way she felt, she wasn't sure she wanted to know.

Danny stirred on the couch.

"Good morning, sunshine." He smiled. "Are you going to be all right?"

Lindsey gunned down two Advils and poured a cup of fresh coffee. "Sorry, Danny. I hated to call you, but there was no way I could drive."

Danny got up and poured himself some coffee. "Not a problem. You know we have an agreement. But I'll tell you, I wish I had shown up about fifteen minutes earlier. You had the crowd captivated with the stories you were telling."

Oh shit, thought Lindsey. "I hate even to ask, but I can barely remember anything from the end of the night. What were the stories I was telling?"

"Well, by the time I got there you were in the middle of a story about the Handelman sisters and the millions of dollars in cash they had," stated Danny. "Even going so far as to say that you were sure it was somewhere on the property. You had found a note saying this and knew the cash had not made it into the banking systems in the area. Your audience of about thirty people was paying close attention."

"Dammit!" Lindsay shouted. "Why do I do that shit? This is not good. Half the population is probably waiting at the gates with shovels. I know better, but it was really wearing on me, and the wine must have let it all loose."

"I wish I could tell you otherwise," said Danny, "but this crowd was dialed in, and you gave them more than they should know. The one thing you did say was that you weren't sure where it was, which may have helped a little. Lindsey, what is the story of this money?"

Lindsey relayed to Danny the discovery of the note and the fact that she and Sheila were going to confront the sisters today to check on this. Danny raised an eyebrow as he digested the unchecked greed and tunnel vision Lindsey was portraying in her description. Although they were friends, sometimes he just didn't like her, and this was one of those times.

Lindsey glanced at the clock to see it was 8:55 a.m. "Danny, I have to get ready as we are meeting Rita and Theresa at eleven this morning. Can you take me back to my car?"

When Danny dropped Lindsey off, he patted her on the shoulder. "Take it easy on them. Is it really worth the stress and worrying since it is not really your money?"

The fiery-eyed look he received said it all as Lindsay waved goodbye and drove back home to get ready for the day.

Lindsey pulled into Sheila Nackers' driveway about ten forty-five and was greeted with a less-than-friendly look. As Sheila entered the car, she asked, "What in the hell were you doing last night? I can't tell you how many text messages I received. Your impromptu drunken presentation has the town buzzing. You may as well have posted a fucking treasure map on Facebook!"

This language coming out of Sheila was rare, so Lindsey knew she was wildly upset. "I am so sorry. This money has just has been wearing on me." She then changed to a questioning tone. "It is a little strange that you would be mad as just yesterday you stated to me that we should probably just let it be. Did you change your mind?"

Sheila responded sadly, "I don't know, Lindsey. You think you don't care or shouldn't be worried about it and yet you are. I don't need the damn money, and neither do you. Would it help us out? Sure, but we are pretty well off without it. I was surprised by how possessive I felt toward that money even though it's not mine. Kind of shameful, really."

Lindsey blasted out, "Shameful, hell! We took care of the sisters for years, and I believe some or all this should be ours. Nobody else deserves it or should have it!"

Here we go again, thought Sheila. "Please take it easy when we get there. Let's go to lunch and verify the will and the other paperwork first. Then we can bring this up when we get back to Handelman Hill."

"Agreed," said Lindsey. "We'll save the talk of the money until we get back."

Rita and Theresa were dressed and ready. Sheila helped them into the car, and the four of them headed west out of town on Highway 70. They settled in at the Riverview Bar and Grill, which was close enough to drive to easily but far enough away from Park Falls to keep the attention level down, which was especially important today. The first order of business was the will. The estimated value of the Handelman sister's assets was near five million dollars, not including the newly discovered cash. This figure included the estate as well as income from investments and proceeds from the sale of the business years ago.

The total would be split evenly between Sheila and Lindsey after honoring the latest addendum, which was to give Paul Handelman $100,000. No other parties were receiving any of the money. The four agreed, but still, there were questions.

Sheila asked as Lindsey glared at her, "Rita and Theresa, did you want to leave anything to the church or charity? Also, what about other relatives such as Paul's sister or children?

Rita replied, "It is good the way it is. We can sign."

At that point, Theresa piped up, "The church will get the other money we have."

Rita made a motion toward her head, telling Lindsey and Sheila that Theresa was making things up. They knew better but left it alone for now. Rita and Theresa signed both copies as well as some power of attorney papers that left Lindsey and Sheila in control.

After lunch, the ladies pulled back into Handelman Hill and stopped in for a cup of coffee. Lindsey presented Rita with the note she had found that stated "$4 million received – GR property." Rita turned pale as she had not expected anyone to find out about this money.

"Where did you get this?"

Lindsey responded, "This was mixed in with your legal papers. There were a lot of other interesting things too, but this one got our attention. Can you shed some light on this? Where is this money? What do you plan on doing with it?"

Rita stammered, "I, I don't know where it is. Dad had it and hid it somewhere. We have never been able to locate it."

Lindsey rose from her seat and walked threateningly toward Rita. "Don't give me that load of shit. I know both of you keep track of everything! Where in the hell is it!"

Rita began to shake, and Theresa stepped in to defend her sister. Despite her Alzheimer's disease, at this moment, she was crystal clear. "It is downstairs, and like I told you it is going to Father Hastings and St. Joseph's Catholic Church."

Lindsey was fuming, and Sheila had to restrain her a bit. "You are giving all that money to the church? Are you crazy? We could use that money. We have taken care of you for years! When I put these papers back in the safe downstairs, I'm going to look for it!"

Rita and Theresa began sobbing a little, and Sheila comforted them. Given her friends' emotional and mental state, she was unsure of where this was going from here. Lindsay grabbed the papers and placed them back in the safe. They could hear her banging around downstairs, cursing as she could not find anything. Finally, she came upstairs, grabbed Sheila, and left, stating on the way out "We'll be back!"

Sheila looked at her friend. "That was smooth. Why didn't you just hit them with a baseball bat while you were at it? Sometimes I don't know about you. Subtlety and patience are certainly not your strong suits."

Lindsey remained silent as she was too disgusted to say anything.

Chapter 10

P aul picked his ringing cell phone off the table and answered as he could see it was Rita.

"Hi, Aunt Rita. Is everything all right?"

Rita replied in a shaky voice, "Paul, can you please stop by this afternoon?"

He did not ask why as Rita rarely called, so there was a good possibility it was serious. "Yes, I'll be over in about fifteen minutes. Sit tight, and I'll be right there."

Driving over, Paul contemplated what might have happened, thinking maybe Theresa was acting out or one of them was injured. Upon arriving, he ran into the kitchen to find Rita and Theresa crying softly while picking up the pieces from the afternoon's debacle.

Rita gave him a big hug. "Oh, Pauly, thank you for coming over! We need to talk to you about something important."

"What is wrong, ladies?" Paul asked, relieved they were not hurt. "My two beautiful aunts usually aren't so distressed. Please tell me how I can help."

Theresa, despite the emotional afternoon, was still dialed in mentally and looked at Paul. "It's the money. Lindsey and Sheila know about the money and that we are going to give it to the church."

Paul wasn't sure if Theresa was bringing up something that actually happened or not, so he gave Rita a look. "You mean your lawyer and banker friends? What did they do?" Although Paul didn't know Lindsey and Sheila personally, he did wonder how trustworthy they were. "Could you please let me know, Rita? Then maybe I can help you."

Rita relayed the events of the afternoon in detail as Paul listened intently.

"We signed that will, but I wish we wouldn't have after the way Lindsey acted this afternoon. They were good to us for years. This money has affected them though."

"Money will do that to people." Paul played along as he tried to process the latest developments including the remark Rita had made about the will. "There was an actual note that said "$4 million received - GR property"? Now that we know there is this money, what can you tell me about it?"

Rita began. "Well, in his later years, your grandfather became infatuated with his Gogebic Range property and wanted to mine it as he discovered some gold there during a test drill. However, he was having trouble with permits and received an unusual offer from a company in Minneapolis. They would pay $250,000 for the land "on the record" and also deliver four million in cash "off the record" as they knew there was gold. This type of transaction would keep the tax burden down and also would not raise any suspicions regarding the usage of the land. It was really out of character for your grandfather to even entertain an offer. However, he accepted and put this money downstairs in a hiding spot, but it seemed to eat away at him the rest of his life. He had regrets for not mining and was never sure what to do with all the cash. It became ours for better or worse when he passed away. Now you know."

Paul's head was spinning with a variety of thoughts, but he kept his emotions in check. This story ran right in line with Tony's research and his own. "Who else knows? Does anyone know exactly where it is?"

Rita responded, "Lindsey, Sheila, and Father Hastings of St. Joseph's know. Only Father Hastings knows where it is along with us. Although Lindsey tried to find it earlier today."

Paul could only imagine what was going through the heads of Lindsey and Sheila right now and suspected they would be pressing the issue very soon. "So what Theresa said is correct? You plan to give all this money to Father Hastings? What makes him so worthy?"

Paul regretted the last question as soon as it flew out of his mouth.

"I mean that's a lot of money for the church. Are you sure that is what you want to do with it?"

Rita replied, "Paul, we just had so many questions about the money. Was it dirty? How would you possibly distribute this and not raise questions? We witnessed what it did to your grandfather, and after he had passed away, we didn't want to think about it, so we let it lay. Now as we are getting older and have some health issues, giving the money to charity seems like a good idea. St. Joseph's Catholic Church and especially Father Hastings have been good to us over the years, so we thought the money could go there."

As a parishioner of St. Joseph's himself, Paul knew Father Hastings and knew the priest would welcome the opportunity to receive this money, but wondered how true his intentions were. At this point, he took out his cellphone and scrolled until he found the picture of the hidden room.

"One more person knows about the location of the money. Me."

Rita raised her hands to her face and let out a gasp. "How did you know?"

Paul relayed the story of the discovery during the furnace check. At this point, the conversation was losing its supportive tone and becoming testy.

"It was quite clever for Grandpa to build this room. I had to look hard to find it and work at it to get in. According to your accounts of this afternoon, it is still hidden well enough as Lindsey did not find it. It's unfortunate no one knew about this money through the years. A lot of people could have been helped in this area. I need to go downstairs and see exactly how much money there is. I am assuming that Father Hastings has not collected yet?"

Rita looked down and stated, "No, no one has been in there, except you of course."

Paul interpreted this as a little white lie as he was sure the priest had been down there. He grabbed his toolbox and proceeded downstairs. Upon opening, the room seemed to be in the same state as last time. Paul carefully picked up the spilled suitcase of money and counted it out as he put it back in place. Five hundred thousand dollars. One by one Paul opened each of the other suitcases. There was truly four million dollars. He then stacked the suitcases up again, this time in groups of four and took another picture as he figured it wouldn't be his last visit to the hidden room.

As the door was sealed, Paul noticed the safe in the back of the furnace room was open a crack. Maybe Lindsey, in her hurry to find the money, had forgotten to lock it. Pulling the door open revealed a stack of papers about three inches high that included his aunt's will as well as other legal documents. Given the developments of the day and Rita's mention of the will, he was very curious to view these documents, so the stack was taken and placed in his toolbox to be looked at later. Before going back upstairs, he closed the safe door to the point where it was before.

Paul entered the kitchen and asked, "Is anyone else coming by tonight or tomorrow outside of your caregivers and me? Do you feel all right, and are you comfortable by yourselves until Jen comes tonight?"

"Nobody is coming by except Jen, and we'll be all right," said Rita. Theresa had not been engaged, lost in thought after her earlier comment.

"The money is there, and your figure is correct. Four million dollars. More people know about this than you would like. For this neck of the woods, it is a fortune and could draw some unwelcome attention. Please lock your doors tight at night and call me if you suspect anything. I believe we should probably put up a security camera soon just for your protection. Tomorrow morning after mass, I am going to have a conversation with Father Hastings to see what his thoughts are about this situation."

Rita and Theresa were silent and not happy. Just a day ago, Father Hastings was the only one who knew about the money, but now it seemed everyone did. Paul was angry, excited, and confused all at once as he gave his aunts a big hug before leaving. What in the hell was going on here? He needed to read these documents very soon. As Paul drove toward town, a thought came to him, and he picked up his phone.

Chapter 11

Around mid-afternoon, Ricky Johnston and two of the Kelley brothers, Justin and Jimmy, entered Tony's Bar and took a seat near the window. This was not their first stop of the day, and they were loud and proud. However, they respected Tony Stenson, and besides, he was way too large of a man to mess with.

Justin called out, "Hey Tony, could you round us up some beer?"

As they stopped in often, Tony brought over two Bud Lights and a Miller Lite.

"What's up today, fellows?" asked Tony with a smile.

"Not much, just a little bar slumming on a beautiful Saturday afternoon," said Ricky.

The group was in their late twenties and typical of a lot of northern Wisconsin men their age, as they had graduated from high school but did not continue their education past that point. Tony felt empathy for this younger generation as the upper Midwest economy had been tough for decades and wasn't getting much better. Upon high school graduation, they basically have two choices. The first was to stay in the area to work a small-town job knowing the economic limitations were very real and options were few. The region had some paper mills as well as some other factories where pay was not great but was enough to make a decent living. However, there always seemed to be a constant fear among the employees that the mill or factory would shut down. Seasonal employment was also available in logging, tourism, and trade jobs such as carpentry or concrete work. The wages were pretty good, but the long Wisconsin winter always brought things to a halt. It seemed half the population was collecting unemployment benefits all winter waiting for the spring.

The second choice was to move from this area for education or a better-paying job in a bigger city, leaving behind this gorgeous piece of the country. It didn't seem fair. Tony always thought that if a company wanted to open up a manufacturing or assembly plant of any type, there were hundreds of Wisconsin towns that had a population to support the labor needs easily. On the rare occasion that a corporation did open a new business in this area, the number of applications for these positions would be ten times the number of job openings. The residents wanted to work for the most part, but there simply weren't enough opportunities. The movement of manufacturing jobs to larger cities or out of the United States had hurt small-town Wisconsin severely.

This led to another troubling trend in this part of the country. It was sad to see, but a lot of fairly able-bodied locals were on disability. It seemed if a person could obtain the counsel of a competent lawyer they could get a pretty decent chunk of money each month for an injury that could be remotely tied to a former job or time in the armed services. While some people were truly in need of these services, Tony suspected most were forced to this option by a lack of money, employment, and hope. He didn't blame them. A man will do what he has to do to feed himself and his family.

Ricky, Justin, and Jimmy all had chosen to stay in the area as they loved it and couldn't imagine living anywhere else. Each was employed and self-sufficient, but money was definitely tight. A three-way conversation started, and Tony's ear was tuned in.

"Can you believe what that lawyer was saying last night at Clancy's?"

"She was smashed out of her mind. Do you really believe that shit? Remember the DA dude came in and gave her a ride home because she was so drunk."

"I'd still like to do her. I don't care if she's almost fifty." All three laughed at this.

"I wasn't paying that much attention, what was she saying?"

"It figures. If you had been listening instead of checking out women's asses, you would have heard her state there was four million dollars in cash up on Handelman Hill!"

"Seriously? They have been secretive up there over the years, and it's definitely a beautiful estate."

"They say the grandfather struck gold in Gogebic Range and went half crazy trying to mine it. Finally, he got disgusted and sold it."

"Plus, he must have had a shitload of money from his business sales. He knew how to make money."

"Where did the cash come from, and where is it?"

"She was a tell-all until that point. Then she pulled her act together and became very vague. That told me she doesn't know. But she seemed damned sure it was there somewhere."

"Boy what we could do with that. That would be like winning the lottery."

Justin got serious. "If I knew where that was, I'd go and get it. Take a chance. We are on a dead-end road up here. I would go after it even at the risk of being caught. That type of money would change a person's life, and my life isn't changing much. Working the same job all week and drinking with you boneheads every weekend. While I'm not complaining, it could be better, and that money would definitely make it better."

Jimmy and Ricky silently contemplated while drinking their beer as they felt the same way. Tony had soaked this all in and now figured he knew why Paul was asking questions yesterday. These three were a little rowdy but still pretty good guys for their age. To hear them talk about risking it all for some money was disheartening, but it accurately reflected the woeful state of life for some of the younger generation that decided to make a northern Wisconsin small town home. Tony imagined that most people around town would also jump at a chance to get this type of money. Given the age of social media, he also suspected most folks would know about this by the end of the day if they didn't know already. His hope was that Paul would come in soon. Otherwise, he would need to get in touch with him.

Chapter 12

Owner Pete Manley picked up the phone on the third ring at Quick Stop Print and Copy in Ladysmith.

"Pete, this is Paul, how the hell are you!"

"Good, Pauly, great to hear from you. What's up?"

The two were good friends from their days in Green Bay. Pete had followed a similar path, retiring up north after selling his printing business, but retirement soon became boring, so he opened a small printing shop, which kept him busy.

Paul was a little rushed. "I have a favor to ask. How late are you open today? I would like to stop by after business hours and make copies of some very important papers."

After a little hesitation, Pete stated, "Open until four, stop by after and we'll see what you have. Sounds important and urgent, so I'll help you out the best I can."

Paul pulled into the shop ten minutes before four and found Pete going through the closing motions as no one else was going to stop by at this time on a beautiful Saturday. The two shook hands and exchanged hellos.

"It's been awhile," said Pete. "What's the story and what do you have to copy?"

Paul responded, "My two aunts are getting up there in age, and I want to get some copies of their will and other documents that they have in their possession. Over the years, Lindsey Barrington, one of the area lawyers, has been running their legal affairs, and I need to see what these documents contain."

Pete was familiar with situations like this, and most of the time he turned down the work, but this was a good friend of his.

"This is the type of stuff that I usually don't do, Pauly. While not illegal, it can get me in trouble as everyone knows everyone else's business up here. Do you know the contents of any of the documents?"

Paul looked down. "I do not know what is in most of these papers, and I'm not sure what I am going to find. I also feel a little sheepish doing this, but there has been a lot of funny business up on Handelman Hill lately, so I need to find out what is there."

Pete locked the door and turned off the Open sign. He grabbed two beers and handed one to Paul.

"Only for you, my friend," he said, smiling. "Lindsey Barrington's reputation is not the best although she's a hell of a defense attorney. I don't blame you for wondering what may be in this stack."

As these were a mix of legal documents and important notes, copying wasn't as simple as feeding them through a machine. Care needed to be taken to line them up properly and select the correct font settings, paper type, and size. So there was no way Pete could copy all this without reading some of it. Since he did not know what Paul knew, he kept most of his thoughts to himself, but it was evident that the general theme of the legal documents was to leave Paul and his family out of most of the money.

Pete delivered the stack of originals and the copies in separate labeled packages.

"Pauly, I didn't read everything there, but I did see some of it during the copy process. I'm not sure how much you already know, but take these documents back to a quiet, private spot before you go over them as I'm not sure you will like everything you see. I will not open the sealed wills, but there were copies along with the official versions, so you should have everything you need."

"Thanks, Pete. Yes, as this moves along, it is getting more bizarre, and you are right, I am not liking what I see. But I need to look at the actual papers to avoid being blindsided anymore."

"Before you leave, Pauly, I do have to ask you one question. There was a handwritten note mixed in that I couldn't help but read before I copied. It said "$4 million received – GR property." Do the ladies actually have that much money at stake?"

Paul picked up the packages, stood up, and shook his friend's hand.

"We would be here half the night if I told you about all the developments over the last couple of days. But yes, there is a lot of money, and I believe that even down in Ladysmith you will hear some of the stories very soon."

"Knowing that I should charge you," joked Pete, "but this one is on the house. Keep in touch and good luck!"

On the drive home, Paul tried to block this all out temporarily and enjoy the beauty of the season as the sun was shining on the end of yet another gorgeous autumn day. He took this in for about ten minutes then realized there were some important phone calls to make, so he broke out his Bluetooth.

Call number one was to Jill, who was out for the day with her friends. Jill picked up and teased, "Hello, stranger, where are you at?"

"On the way home from Ladysmith. Drove over to see Pete Manley to get some copies made. How was your day?"

"Excellent. Met the gang for lunch and did some shopping together. Right now, I'm just putting the finishing touches on dinner, so I'm happy you are on the way."

"Did you hear anything regarding Theresa and Rita while you were around town today?"

"There was some talk of money, but there is always that it seems. Why do you ask, and what were you getting copied up at Pete's?"

"Well, if you thought yesterday was exciting, wait until you hear about today. I will let you know when I get home. In the meantime, can you look up Father Hastings' phone number for me? I need to give him a call."

"Sure, I'll text it over. You have me worried now. Should I be?"

"I don't think you should be worried, but this just became a lot more complicated. Love you and see you in a bit. I need to make that call."

Next on the list was Rita, who sounded a bit scared when she picked up on the second ring.

"Hello, this is Rita."

"Hi, Rita, this is Paul. Is everything going okay? Would you like me to stop by?"

"Oh, Paul, thanks for calling, but we are doing fine. Jen is cooking dinner now. We are doing good, I will call you if we need anything, but I know you are busy too."

Paul thought to himself that another thing elderly people did either by design or without knowing is play the "you are busy too" card. What this usually meant is they would like you to stop but could understand if you didn't. Depending on how busy you truly were, you would feel guilty at times. No guilt was felt today.

"Yes, I had a busy day, and we do have a lot going, so I am on the way home. Just thought I would check in, and remember, I will be over tomorrow afternoon for my Sunday visit."

"Thanks for everything, Paul, we'll see you tomorrow."

One word that would describe his aunts would be resilient as they were very good at moving on with life even after tough days like today. He was thankful for that.

Paul pulled off on a scenic overview parking lot just off the highway. With the trees turning colors and sun setting, the view facing west was magnificent. There were several other people in the lot taking this in, so he got out of the car, stretched, and joined them to enjoy the scenery for a few minutes. Then he climbed back in and broke out the telephone number that Jill had given him. As he dialed, he was prepared to get voice mail as Father Hastings was a busy man and probably had just finished up with Saturday afternoon mass.

As the beep of the voice mail faded, Paul left his message: "Hi, Father Hastings, this is Paul Handelman. On a visit with my aunts Rita and Theresa today, they stated that they would like to give some of their money to the church and you. They were a little shy on details, and as they are getting along in age, I would like to meet with you to discuss. I know that you are busy with Mass until 11:00 a.m. Sunday, but I would like to get together at eleven forty-five if possible. I will come to your house. If you are unable to make this time, please call my cell phone. I'll see you tomorrow morning. Thank you."

About ten minutes into the remaining leg of his drive home, Paul received a call from Tony Stenson as the conversation he had heard that afternoon was wearing on him.

"Paul, this is Tony. Today a group of my regular boys stopped in and began discussing how Lindsey Barrington held court at Clancy's on Friday night. She told everyone within earshot that there was money on Handelman Hill, although she didn't say where."

Paul sighed deeply. "What else can happen today? Now you know the reason for my visit yesterday. This is turning into a soap opera. I'm sure the entire town will know by the end of the day. Thanks for letting me know, Tony. I was busy and didn't hear that one yet. When this settles down a bit, I'll stop in and fill in the blanks for you. I appreciate your support, buddy."

Tony replied, "No problem, Paul. I didn't know when I would see you next, so I thought I'd get in touch. Let me know if I can help you in any way. I'll keep my ears open."

Paul was sure Tony would.

"Thanks, Tony, we'll see you soon." *Just another ring to add to the circus*, he thought as he shook his head.

Paul arrived home and walked into the house with his packages from Pete where he found Jill sitting by the fireplace with a glass of wine. Dinner was ready, but it would be on hold tonight. Paul grabbed a beer out of the refrigerator and joined her to pass on the events of the day, including Lindsey's visit, the counting of the money, the copying of the legal papers, and the phone call from Tony.

Jill looked at him with wide eyes. "Tell me this is not true. I thought things were complicated yesterday. This is a whole new level. I don't even know what to say. I'm glad we are going up to Lake Superior Sunday night for a few days. Maybe we can regroup. This is taking over our lives, and I'm not liking it!"

Paul gave her a look, and Jill responded, "Don't even think about not going, especially with everything else happening here. This is something you and I need right now. Bring the papers along, and we can spend some time looking at them. As Pete mentioned, you should find a quiet spot."

"I agree," said Paul. "I just worry about the ladies with all this going on. But I do need some quiet time to sort through it all. Another piece of the puzzle will be coming tomorrow when I meet with Father Hastings. This is crazy."

Chapter 13

Sunday morning dawned cold and gray, bringing an abrupt end to the summerlike weather the region had been experiencing. This was the other side of October's spectrum, sending out a warning that winter was just around the corner. Paul poured a cup of coffee and sat by the patio door in the dining room silently observing the somewhat opaque outside world. He would not be going to church this morning as his mind was too preoccupied thinking about the meeting with Father Hastings at eleven forty-five.

Paul considered himself a good Christian as he led his life as the Lord would want by helping others, acting kind, and being a decent person. Most would not consider him a "practicing Christian" as he attended church just on occasion. Where that left him in the big scheme of things was unknown, but he was generally comfortable with it. Paul thought it was a waste of time to attend church services unless you were able to immerse your mind and your soul into the proceedings. If a person had other thoughts going through their head, there were many junctures during a Catholic mass to get lost in those thoughts and never catch the message, so what was the point of going?

A Catholic school in Green Bay provided Paul's education up to the eighth grade, meaning masses five days a week during the school year, plus Sunday with his family. He had also served as an altar boy and completed all of his Catholic sacraments. At one time, he was pretty sure he could have delivered mass as the ceremony was very structured and hadn't changed much over the years. Maybe the number of church services attended as a child also contributed to his lack of interest at this stage in his life.

The priests Paul had met through the years were rock solid, dedicated, and very respectable human beings for the most part. However, some had issues with alcohol, and others had "housekeepers" with whom they became very involved. Even though they were men of God, the priests were still men and had the same physical, mental, and emotional needs. He often wondered why the Vatican would not allow them to marry as his belief was that it would have helped them become better men and would also have given them a better grip on marriage counseling having to walk the walk themselves.

Father James Hastings had been at St. Joseph's for quite a few years, and Paul became acquainted with him through attending masses with his aunts, and more recently with Jill. Father Hastings was a little more boisterous and dramatic than most priests, which led to some fire-and-brimstone homilies, but Paul wondered whether he believed everything he said. His suspicion was that Father Hastings was not 100 percent committed to the priesthood, but Paul could not come up with a solid reason why. It was just a hunch based on human observation of the priests he had known over his lifetime. As Paul poured himself another cup of coffee, he started to wonder how this generous gift from his aunts to the church ever got started. Hopefully, some answers would come today.

At promptly 11:45 a.m., Paul knocked on the front door of Father Hastings' small ranch-style home, which was right next to the St. Joseph's Catholic Church. The priest answered the door in a somewhat subdued voice.

"Good morning, Paul. Please come in and sit down. I didn't see you at mass today."

Paul entered the cozy living room and sat on one end of the couch. "Thank you, Father. No, I did not attend today. A lot of thoughts are going through my head right now."

Father Hastings offered coffee and some doughnuts. "I must say I was a little surprised by your message yesterday, but we can certainly talk. It was my understanding that the arrangement between your aunts and me was private."

Paul accepted a cup of coffee and took a sip. "It may have been private until a couple of days ago. There were a lot of developments. Let's just say a lot of people probably have heard of this money by now."

Father Hastings asked, "How did you find out about the money?"

It was time Paul took over as the inquisitor, so he changed the direction. "That can be discussed later. Please tell me everything you know about this gift that my aunts promised the church."

Father recognized the switch and complied. "A couple of years ago Rita and Theresa asked for advice on donating to the church. They wanted to know if they could give cash and also if it was necessary to wait until they both passed away. I told them we could take donations anytime and would be open to whatever they would like to do including taking it in anonymously. Then they told me the story about the cash they had inherited as part of their father's estate. I didn't believe it completely until they invited me over one day recently and showed me where it was. Obviously, a gift like that could do wonders for our parish and its members."

And it would do wonders for you also, Paul thought. "So you know how much money there is? And you have no qualms about taking that sum of money when some of it could be used elsewhere to help people?"

The salesman in Father Hastings awoke. "Paul, what would be a better spot to leave that money than the church? We would take care of our debt and help out our families in need. It would be a wonderful gift for our parish, which would help many people for years to come. Yes, I do know the amount as I counted it myself."

"What would Father Hastings do if he had this money? Where would you keep it? This is not the amount of money you can put in the bank without drawing attention. But if you don't, you have a lot of cash hanging around and no audit trail."

The priest was getting a little impatient. "Where is this going, Paul? This seems to be a decision your aunts have made, which we will execute soon. I'm not sure you have too much to say about it.

Rita and Theresa have been in touch lately and talked about starting to distribute."

"I may not have much to say about it, but I do take care of my aunts, and I also know where the money is," stated Paul as he produced the picture of the hidden room on his phone. As the priest looked at the picture, Paul also told him about the phone call from Tony and the fact the entire town probably knew by now.

Father Hastings had not expected this. "How did you find this, and what do you plan on doing?"

Paul told Father Hastings the story of the crashing suitcase and his discovery of the room. "I'm not sure what I plan on doing. It just doesn't feel right that all this money should go to you and the parish. I just wanted to talk with you about it. It seems you think it would be best if St. Joseph's received all this money, and I don't agree."

Father Hastings closed by saying, "Paul, I think this conversation has run its course. Look to the Lord for guidance and peace. Rita and Theresa will decide what is best."

Paul respectfully shook hands with the priest and politely said goodbye.

Jill was making lunch as Paul entered the house.

"Well, how did that go?"

"He wants the money, that's for sure. He was surprised that I and others knew about it and that I knew exactly where the cash was. That made him a little anxious. I could see Father Hastings collecting the money and retiring soon after. It makes me sick. I can't put a finger on it, but I don't think he has good intentions. Not once did he listen when I suggested that other charities in the area could use it. That certainly was not the action of a Christian let alone a good Catholic priest. I'm half tempted to pull it out myself and bring it home."

Jill gave him a look. "Oh, that would be great. Basically, steal four million dollars from your aunts and keep it here? I am hoping you are joking. However, I hear what you are saying about Father Hastings. I notice that too, just a general lack of commitment at times. It seems he longs to be elsewhere and is not entirely devoted to the church or his flock."

After lunch, Paul drove over to Handelman Hill as he needed to move the garbage and recyclable material to their spots for Monday morning pickup. He also quickly ran downstairs and placed the legal documents back in the safe before stopping in for a visit.

"Aunt Rita, do you have a cold Miller Lite in the fridge? I'm thirsty today." Paul smiled.

This put his aunts at ease a little bit as they were not sure how the conversation would go this afternoon after yesterday.

"Jill and I will be leaving for a few days starting today as I promised her a short trip up to northern Minnesota. We have a spot on the Knife River by Lake Superior where we will spend a few days alone. Given the events of the week, we could use the time together. You have my cell phone, and if anything arises, I can be back in about three hours."

Rita replied, "That is fine, Paul, we are used to you not stopping over every day. The caretakers will be in and out, so please enjoy your time together. Did you meet with Father Hastings as you intended to?"

Paul started to review the events of his meeting.

"I met with him today, and he mentioned that both of you had talked to him about this money and it was almost a sealed deal that this would go to St. Joseph's. I asked Father Hastings if he thought that maybe it could be distributed to other charities in the area as well, but he was adamant that St. Joseph's should be the recipient. He also became irritable and anxious when I mentioned that I knew where the money was as well. He told me to trust in the Lord and that you would make the right decision."

The sisters, at ease no longer, sat in silence listening, so Paul continued.

"I'll be honest with you. I am not happy that St. Joseph's is getting all this money. Jill and I are in good shape financially, but there seems to be a fairness element here that was never addressed. Your brother Joe, my father, was alive and well when this money was obtained. As Father Hastings relayed to me, you had stated that you received this as part of the estate. If that was so, why didn't my father receive any of this money?"

Rita was starting to shake a little. "Paul, it was agreed to give this money to the church. Right now, I am ready to start it on fire I'm so sick of talking about it! There were a lot of agreements over the years as your grandfather helped your dad financially so he could expand his business. This is where we sit today, and I would truly like to get rid of this cash soon."

Paul picked up the obvious that his aunts were upset, so he backed off. "All right, we'll leave it at that. But there are a lot of people who know about this now. That is my primary concern. Even if you give this all to St. Joseph's, it won't become public knowledge, so the rumors will persist, which may put you in harm's way. We will have to put some security cameras in and reinforce some of the locks. Don't take this the wrong way, but you have both grown up in an environment where money was never a concern. There was always plenty of it, and having enough never entered your mind. That is far from the norm up here. Most people in this area worry a lot about having enough money to survive day to day.

"Just look down Old Horseshoe Road at some of the ramshackle homes and beat-up trailers that people live in. This type of money would dramatically change the lifestyle of 95 percent of the people up here, and that is why I am a little concerned. Please think about what you will be doing with the money, and I also believe it should be made public somehow when you disburse it, which would minimize the attention. I will call a time or two over the next couple of days just to check in if you don't mind."

Paul gave them each a hug and kiss before he left. He was getting tired of the cash also, and the trip to Lake Superior would be a welcome diversion.

Chapter 14

Just past Handelman Hill around the far corner of Old Horseshoe Road sat five acres of property now owned by Jerry Basten. On it sat a trailer house, an old pole building, and several rusted cars that hadn't run in years. The Bastens were a statewide headline back in 2011 when federal, state, and local authorities exposed a rather large-scale methamphetamine lab. Jerry, his brother Tommy, and their dad Bill all went to trial separately after pleading not guilty. Bill was up for trial first and was sent to the big house for twenty years. After this, the boys turned on their father and, with the help of their defense attorney, Lindsey Barrington, were able to get away with probation.

Tommy counted his blessings and moved to Montana once his probation was up. Jerry continued to live in the area but was unable to find anything except temporary employment due to his past criminal activities. He cleaned up his act out of necessity as the local and state police made frequent visits to his home to make sure there were no reoccurring illegalities. As the frustration mounted for Jerry over the years, his drinking increased, and at present, he was a full-fledged alcoholic. Unable to find work, he collects welfare along with his live-in girlfriend, Brenda Jennings, and can be found at one of the country taverns within a ten-mile radius of their home drinking seventy-five-cent tap beers nearly every day between mid-morning and late afternoon.

As the couple sat in Blondie's Pub on Highway 70 Sunday afternoon, they heard the rumor of the Handelman Hill money. Even though they lived only a half mile away, their worlds could not have been more different, and truthfully, Jerry knew very little about his country neighbors. It did not surprise him that there was talk of this money as even the stupidest ass could see by looking at their estate that the Handelmans were loaded. The story was interesting though as they were talking about millions of dollars in cash, and Jerry had a lot of experience with large sums of money from his past life, so he was dialed in.

Their drinking buddy Frankie Taylor was telling the story.

"I stopped in at Tony's Bar in Park Falls yesterday, and I overheard the story of the money from the Kelley boys who were discussing what they had heard on Friday night. From what I understand, Lindsey Barrington spilled her guts about four million dollars in cash that is up at Handelman Hill."

Jerry just about spit out his beer as he was laughing.

"Lindsey Barrington? That's the lawyer bitch that got me probation at my trial. After the old man was convicted, I thought I was fucked, but she came up with a great defense and somehow got Tommy and me off with probation. Not sure what makes her tick as we were nothing but low-lifers, but she made it her mission to free us. It seems she likes to stir the pot a little when it comes to authority. What exactly did she say?"

Frankie continued. "I texted a few guys in town also just to confirm some of this. She insisted the money was there in the form of cash but did not say where. I would guess she probably doesn't know. Otherwise, she would have taken it. From what I understand, she was extremely drunk though, so who knows. Just the two old biddy aunts are living there now although they have a lot of help coming in and out of the place. You live right there, what do you see, Jerry?"

"Not much," stated Jerry as he downed his beer. "We drive by but never had a reason to stop in. Just like everyone else, the Handelmans know about our past life and avoid us, I'm sure. It's just the two old ladies there now anyway. She didn't say anything about where the money might be?"

"No," said Frankie. "She was very shy with the details. I am going to keep my ears open around town though. That's a lot of fucking money."

"That is a shitload of cash. I have half a notion to call Lindsey, but she won't want to remember me," stated Jerry. "Maybe we can scout around there some night. I wonder if they have it buried somewhere? We could certainly use a helping hand in our lives. I can't find a job to save my soul, and money is tight all the time. Give it some thought, where would you put that kind of money if you had it?"

Frankie asked, "Where did you put yours at the time?"

"I'm thinking back," said Jerry. "We scattered it all over the place. I think the Handelmans are more organized than we were. It sounds like it was there for a while too. I would guess they either buried it somewhere or have it hidden inside the house."

Frankie laughed. "No shit, Sherlock, you're a fucking genius! Either outside or inside." Jerry and Brenda broke out laughing and flagged Blondie over to pour all three of them another beer.

Chapter 15

The A-frame loft Jill and Paul rented just north of the Knife River had an east side that faced Lake Superior made up almost entirely of windows. On a sunny morning, the view was stunning. As they woke up Monday morning, a cold northeast wind blew through a cloud-filled sky, sending huge waves crashing along the beach. As every seasoned sailor or fisherman knew, the Great Lakes were temperamental and could change from calm to stormy on a minute's notice. Superior was especially cantankerous today with the wind howling from a northerly direction, and Paul imagined it was probably churning like this when the great freighter *The Edmund Fitzgerald* went down back in November of 1975. The couple shared a peaceful breakfast as they witnessed the big lake roil.

The drive up on Sunday evening had been uneventful and quiet as both seemed lost in thought over the events of the last few days. Paul rose to get some more coffee.

"Well, looks like this is a terrible day to hike or even to go to town. Don't get mad at me, but would it be all right if I went through those papers this morning? I slept decently last night and am pretty fresh."

Jill responded, "That's fine. I can help you. I just worry about what you might find in there. You need to promise to go about this methodically, take notes, and keep the emotions at bay. If you can do that, we can go through them."

Paul leaned over and gave Jill a kiss. "Of course, thanks. I am expecting some things will not be to my liking, so we'll just sort through the papers and take notes as you stated."

The first pass involved categorizing the documents. When they finished, there were four stacks. The Handelman sisters' will, Gogebic Range property, Robert Handelman's will—which they did not expect to find, and a pile of "other" documents that included home improvement receipts as well as paid receipts for lawyers and other service professionals. The ladies were record keepers by trade, so it was not surprising that they held on to papers of all types, but Paul wasn't sure how much of it would be valuable.

"Interesting already. Let's start with the "other" pile just to see if there is anything worth noting."

The first thing they ran into was a detailed log of payments to Lindsey Barrington and Sheila Nackers. They were both collecting $200 per month for their work on financial and legal matters. The receipts went all the way back to 2001. Keeping emotions in check was being tested right out of the gate for Paul as this seemed excessive for the little bit of service work they did. What did the ladies need at this point? Maybe the companionship was that valuable? It seemed like a profitable gig for Lindsey and Sheila.

The second set of items involved the sale of Handelman Wood Products by his two aunts in 1995, four years after their father died. The sale price was $2.7 million dollars. Paul took a deep breath and wondered if his father Joe was ever part of this conversation. The rest of the papers in the "other" stack were mainly home improvement invoices for Handelman Hill. Paul did make a note of one item. There was a receipt for the "remodeling of the storage room," which included a door and wall addition. This work was completed in 1989 by a local carpenter named James Olsen. So it appeared his grandfather did not build the hidden room until after he received the money.

Next, Paul and Jill reviewed the Gogebic Property stack. Front and center was the short handwritten note "$4 million received - GR property."

"Here it is," stated Paul.

Jill responded, "I wonder why they thought it was necessary to have this note among their legal papers. Do you think it was an oversight?"

"Not sure," said Paul. "Here is a copy of the official property purchase and sale, which matches exactly with the records in the courthouse. Both my grandfather and my aunts were very meticulous record keepers, but I'm not sure why they thought it valuable to keep this note. Maybe it was a mistake. That's all that is there for the Gogebic Range property. No surprise there, at least not now."

Jill motioned to the last two stacks. "Which would you like to look at next?"

"Let's look at the will of Rita and Theresa," said Paul. "Uncovering my grandfather's will was unexpected, so we'll save that for last."

Once Paul got through the legal jargon, his aunts' will was very simple. Nothing was being left to his sister or his children. Lindsey Barrington and Sheila Nackers were the executors with instructions to sell everything including the Handelman Hill estate. There was an addendum from last year, which included Paul for $100,000. The rest of the money would be split between Lindsey and Sheila.

Paul rose from his chair, slammed the copy of the will on the table, and walked toward the window.

"I'm not sure how much more I can go through, Jill. I feel like I've been slapped in the face by my own family. Doesn't money of that kind usually stay in the family? These two bloodsuckers have attached themselves to Rita and Theresa and planned to clean the estate out. Then to top it off, that's not enough for Barrington. She needed to turn the basement upside down trying to find the cash! Given what they've been paid over the years, it's appalling that they would have the nerve to take that kind of money from my aunts!"

"Paul, how innocent do you think your aunts are?" asked Jill, who was a little agitated. "You don't know all that much about them other than that they had a mysterious past. Plus, you must have half expected this. Lindsey and Sheila were with your aunts for a couple of decades. I imagine they slowly paved their way into the hearts and souls of the ladies. Our girls rarely if ever stop to visit them, and your sister and her family never do, so there is no surprise there. You were probably not part of the picture until the last year or so, but they love you enough to include you. Again, please look at this objectively and keep your emotions out of it! At least until we get through everything."

Paul silently made a few notes regarding the will and then moved to the final set, which included his grandfather's will and related documents. It took Paul and Jill a good thirty minutes to piece through the papers to come up with their conclusion. When Robert Handelman died, the company and any other assets went to Rita and Theresa. Paul's dad, Joseph, was left out of his grandfather's final will. There was a signed paper from the 1970s that stated Robert Handelman would gift $120,000 to Joseph Handelman for use in expanding his business in Green Bay.

The price Paul's father paid for this gift was to sign off on any further asset transfers during Robert's life and after he died. Paul put his head in his hands for a moment, then stated, "Okay, we are through this, and I understand the facts. I guess I'll never know or understand the reason Grandpa shortchanged my father. Does it all go back to the fact that he didn't want anything to do with the family business? What a heavy load of stress he must have carried knowing he left this behind."

"I'm not sure about that," responded Jill. "Your dad needed that money at the time to expand out his auto repair facilities in Green Bay knowing full well that you would probably join him and together you would become very successful. And here's the key, this would be without your grandfather presiding over everything. I would guess your father was very content with his decision as it was a one-time gift that broke all financial ties with your grandfather and the obligatory control that came with it. He was now his own man and finally could do what he did best without any restraints. It worked well for your grandfather also as he felt he was punishing your father and helping him at the same time. Just the kind of response I believe Robert Handelman would want as we get to know his actions a little better with each passing day. I would guess your father was experiencing a lot of stress before he took this action, not after."

"You may be right," Paul whispered. Then he rose from his chair. "We have four million dollars in cash going to a half-committed Catholic priest if someone else in town does not run across it first. Also, there is about 2 to 2.5 million each going to the lawyer and banker who were compensated for their services over the years. However, we do get $100,000 when they pass away. Did you ever wish you could turn back the clock and not discover or experience something? This is one of those times. Where are we with this, and what do we need to do?"

It had been a long, testy morning, and the weather was not getting any better outside.

"Let's have some lunch and take a nap." Jill smiled.

"Sounds good," said Paul. "I am worn out. When we wake, maybe we can go into town."

About 4:30 p.m., the two of them finally arose.

"Wow, I guess we were tired," Paul said as he smiled. "I think we are just flat-out exhausted from the last week's events. Not hard to understand. Seriously, I could just stay here and watch the big lake instead of going out in this weather. Tomorrow will probably be better."

"Sure, we have plenty to eat and drink. Let's start a fire, have some drinks, and enjoy the evening," replied Jill.

The wine and other spirits were flowing freely as was the talk, and soon Paul became philosophical.

"Jill, can you tell me why I care about this money? Why do people give so much thought to becoming rich or figuring out who gets what assets? I accused my aunts of not knowing what it is like to be in need of money. The truth of the matter is that I don't know either. I had a great childhood and then went into business with my father. There was never a time when I wondered where my next dollar was coming from. When we sold the business, we received enough money to help our kids out and be very comfortable for the rest of our lives.

"And yet, I feel attached to this money that is my aunts'. Why? Money truly can be an evil thing as it rules your thoughts and influences your actions. Why should I give a shit if Father Hastings gets four million dollars and runs off to the Caribbean with his housekeeper? Why should I care if Lindsey Barrington and Sheila Nackers are the beneficiaries of my aunts' will? And yet, it consumes me as you witnessed today. I have done nothing over the last four or five days that did not involve that money. I've pissed off my aunts and the parish priest all in the name of what? The care I give to Rita and Theresa has suffered, and my heart is not where it was before. After reading all that shit today, I'm not sure where I am at."

"All I know is that I want my husband back," replied Jill. "I'm not sure who this crusader for the four million dollars is with his superhero cape making sure the money goes the right way. That is certainly not my husband. He is a man of strong character who does the right thing and really is comfortable in his own skin. Paul, this money is truly eating you up. You've hit on some good points. We don't need it, and why should we care who gets it? I was tied up in it for a little while too, so I gave you some space, but the last couple of days took the cake. Stealing the legal documents for a short time and making copies as well as making it known you do not approve of the arrangement between your aunts and the church. This is not the Paul I know."

Paul sat silent for a minute or so and became misty-eyed.

"Jill, I am so sorry. Reflecting back, I am not sure what came over me, but you are right. What business is it of mine where this money goes? I help the ladies out of the goodness of my heart and because I love them, not because I want four million dollars. They will need me more than ever now, and yet I let this money get in the way. I am so ashamed. I have a wonderful family, the best wife a husband could ask for, my health, and enough resources to live comfortably. What a lucky man I am! Yet my judgment was clouded by greed, anger, and resentment. These are things that have never occupied a minute of my time, yet I became weak enough to let them consume my life for the better part of a week. Thank you for being patient and listening. You have your husband back. I can't tell you how much I love you."

Chapter 16

As he rose from kneeling on the altar in the empty church, Father James Hastings gave the crucifix hanging in the middle of St. Joseph's a good, long look. Monday had been a day of reflection for him, and he was no closer to reconciliation of any kind than before. He had always been a conflicted human being, but the calling to serve the Lord had won out over many others. Early on, Father Hastings thought the priesthood would steady his wanderlust as the Lord's work would require his time and concentration. However, there were always nagging temptations and dreams hanging out there that he wanted to pursue. To his credit, Father kept following the straight and narrow to the best of his abilities.

Tall, handsome, and now in his fifties, he reflected on his life. By anyone's standards, it had been a good one as he had served the Lord well in several different Catholic parishes. However, those on the outside did not understand the loneliness and the longing for things other men freely acquired with no consequence. Catholic priests were trained to embrace these challenges and trust in Jesus Christ, but sometimes it was tough. The opportunity presented to him by Rita and Theresa Handelman had truly thrown him into a quandary.

"Lord, I have served you well," began Father Hastings as he gazed at the crucifix. "How will you judge me if I accept this money to use for the parish and myself? What if I left the priesthood? What would you think? I have been your faithful servant for my whole life, but you know that I have faults and desire other things. Is it necessary for a priest to serve his entire life once he commits to you? Or is it acceptable to resume a life that doesn't involve the priesthood? How will you judge me?"

Then Father Hastings knelt down and prayed some more. The thought of leaving the priesthood had been intense about fifteen years ago also, when a good friend of his, Joseph Renardi, left to get married and raise a family. At the time, he also considered this option but after weeks of prayer and reflection decided to stay the course. A few years later he was transferred to tranquil St. Joseph's Parish with its beautiful nineteenth-century architecture and a loving, faithful membership. His love of the outdoors and small-town life made it a perfect fit. He settled in nicely and became friends with most of his parish members, including Rita and Theresa Handelman.

About two years ago, the ladies told Father Hastings about the money they had at the estate. Once the cash was actually viewed, he began to unravel again as thoughts of leading another life returned with a vengeance. His imagination ran wild thinking of what he could do with this money and the lifestyle he could lead. He had served the Lord for enough time, right? In his mind, no one would think badly of him, and he deserved this in so many ways.

"Lord, the expectations of your servants are high," began the priest. "When you get right down to the point, we are men who have wants and desires that are the same as other men have. We are tempted as other men are but dare not entertain the thought of such actions. Yet we spend our time alone. Was this the design you had in mind for those that spread the Word of God in your name? Were we to be denied pleasures of the common man just to deliver the Word of the Lord?"

Father Hastings' voice rose in volume.

"I have been enticed in the past and am now at temptation's door again. How do I reconcile, my Lord? I know your expectation, but I grow weaker in my faith instead of stronger as each year of my life passes. As your humble servant, I ask for your guidance and your forgiveness. Amen."

The priest prayed silently for ten minutes and then bowed toward the crucifix before walking out of the church to his house next door. The Handelman money was tearing him up inside. It was like two people were fighting it out. He did not see them as good or evil but viewed them as options. Does he accept the money and the potential guilt that comes with it when a new life is started? Or does he remain steadfast and encourage the ladies to spread the wealth out to various charities in the area? It was a real paradox that was sorely testing his faith, and at this time Father Hastings wasn't at all sure how this would end up.

Chapter 17

M a and Pa's Bakery, located on the south end of Main Street in Park Falls, was a hopping place Monday morning despite the cold and rainy weather. John Chervek and his wife Louise started the establishment in 1948 as a simple takeout bakery. Their philosophy was to consistently offer a quality product at a fair price, and the baked goods were known throughout northwest Wisconsin. John was formally educated only up to the third grade but had a doctorate in common sense. He passed this gift on to his son Charles who along with his wife, Kathy, took over the business in 1985. Both couples were known to the locals affectionately as Ma and Pa.

Kathy brought an entrepreneurial spirit to the business and incorporated several changes over the years. They bought the other half of the building in which they did business and set up several tables so people could enjoy their doughnuts and visit. The big money maker she brought in was higher-end coffee. On a trip to Minneapolis, she noticed several establishments offering better-quality coffee at some relatively high prices. When she proposed the idea to Pa, he was skeptical, but they gave it a try. It was a huge success, and like Pa said, "If they want to keep paying 2.99 for their coffee, I'll keep making it." The bakery was now a favorite gathering spot for retired folks as well as those on their way to work looking for top-of-the-line baked goods and coffee served with the latest small-town gossip.

Ma and her staff did most of the food preparation while Pa made coffee, watched over the orders, and kept an ear open for the latest rumors. He was hearing it today as there was an unending supply of stories involving Handelman Hill and the money. Pa thought he heard four million dollars in cash but wasn't sure. There was talk of the money being buried somewhere on the property and every other imaginable spot. When you combine a small town and millions of dollars, the stories know no bounds. Pa waited until the morning crowd wound down and then took a seat by his friend, everyday regular Mike Gunther.

"Holy shit, Mike, the rumors are flying," said Pa. "I wasn't able to pay much attention, so can you fill me in?"

"Not paying attention to gossip is not one of your issues." Mike laughed. "But there was a lot of it today. The way I understand it, Lindsey Barrington shot her mouth off at Clancy's Friday night stating there was money at Handelman Hill for sure, but she didn't know where, which makes sense because if she did know we wouldn't be having this conversation."

"She would know the details as the Handelman lawyer," stated Pa. "This could get interesting as the ladies are getting up there in age."

"I just hope they are well protected and that the money is in a safe spot," responded Mike. "Every yahoo within fifty miles has heard some version of the story by now. Money doesn't come easy in the north, and I fear what some of these people would do. Well, I need to get going, Pa. We'll see you tomorrow as usual."

Around mid-morning, Josie Waters stopped by for doughnuts and coffee. The few people left in Ma and Pa's gave her some looks as she was Lindsey Barrington's paralegal. Knowing most of what was happening, she thanked Ma for the goods with a smile and left promptly.

Pa walked back into the kitchen. "Have you heard any of those conversations today? It's insane. That is all people are talking about."

Ma replied, "Yes, even back here we heard. I hope the ladies will be all right. No telling what some of these people around here might do for that kind of money."

Lindsey Barrington was still furious about the money but was unsure what to do about it. A big problem was not knowing the location of the cash. Knowing that others were getting it was the real issue though. She had been the village idiot over the weekend, but it was now Monday, and soon someone else would play the fool, so that didn't bother her. Lindsey was just hoping no one else would be making their way to Handelman Hill this week to inquire, invited or uninvited.

As these thoughts rolled around in her mind, she called Josie over, and they began prepping for a court case she had on Friday. Lindsey was thankful for this as she would be occupied all week with the case work, which would not allow her to spend time thinking about the money. At times like these work was a good thing.

Sheila Nackers arrived at the office facing another busy week, which was good for her also as there would not be a lot of time to reflect on the nightmarish events of the weekend. She had unloaded on Lindsey and rightfully so. Sheila genuinely liked the Handelman sisters and did not appreciate how her friend had treated them. She felt a little uncomfortable about even being in the will at all but had found peace with this and the four million dollars over the weekend.

Sheila was currently divorced and spent her time at work or with her two adult children and families in the area, activities which she enjoyed very much. On Sunday, she took a life inventory and determined that she was okay with whatever came her way regarding any of this money. However, she would not push the issue and also would not object if things changed and she was left out. The cash seemed to be causing a great deal of stress for the Handelman sisters and everyone else that knew about it, including her.

There was one problem, and that was Lindsey who would want to go after the four million dollars as soon as possible. This idea seemed insane to Sheila as they didn't even know where it was and were already in the sisters' will. But Lindsey was a maverick, so it virtually guaranteed there would be some movement soon. She called her to gauge the potential actions and was relieved to hear that she had a busy week ahead and wouldn't be able to do much of anything except court preparation. You can't buy time, but this did not hurt.

The Lord knew that everyone needed a cooling-off period after the weekend.

Jimmy Kelley entered the break room at GLK Industries in Park Falls around 11:30 a.m. with the rest of his thirty coworkers. There was no doubt what the topic of conversation would be during this lunch break. One of his buddies spoke up first.

"Jimmy, did you really hear that story in person Friday night?"

"Yes, I was at Clancy's with Justin and Ricky. She was telling everyone there was money somewhere up on Handelman Hill but didn't say where."

Another coworker piped in, "You know what I would do if I found that money? I would buy this place and fire all your asses!"

The break room roared with laughter, and the rest of the time was spent by everyone dreaming out loud of what they could do with that kind of cash, not surprising considering the workers made $12–14 per hour for their labor.

As Lisa Morris pulled onto Old Horseshoe Road on her way to provide care for Rita and Theresa, she noticed more traffic than usual. When she pulled through the gated entrance of Handelman Hill, she could see why. More than one car was parked or driving by slowly gawking at the estate. Since Lisa didn't live under a rock, she too had heard the stories from the weekend. She vowed to keep an eye out and would probably call the sheriff if there were still a lot of cars when her shift ended at noon. It seemed even the person who did live under the rock had heard about the money.

Chapter 18

Despite the heavier than usual traffic on Old Horseshoe Road earlier in the day, Lisa had monitored throughout the morning, and by the time she left around noon, the flow was back to normal, which consisted of an occasional car going one direction or the other. Hopefully, this trend would continue, and the curiosity would be short-lived. Unfortunately, Theresa's dementia was increasing at a rapid pace.

She cried out, "I want Mom. Where is my mom? I need her to help me."

Rita replied as convincingly as she could, "I'm here to help you, Theresa. What is wrong? What do you need? Mom is not here right now."

"Mom is the only one that can help me. I saw her last night. She is there for me. You are my sister, right?"

"Oh, Theresa, yes, I am your sister," said Rita, now crying a little. "I will help you the best I can."

"I know, you were there when I fell off the swing and hurt my ankle. You helped me. I need Mom now. I have lost everything. I don't know where anything is. I saw her last night, and I want to be with her. I am scared!"

Rita gave her a big hug. "I am here for you while Mom is away. I will help you."

"Just let me know when she gets back. I need her and want to be with her."

Theresa sat on the chair, sipped her glass of water, and remained silent. Rita took a deep breath. This Alzheimer's disease was terrible. Just two months ago Theresa was able to do most everything and could remember day-to-day activities. Lately, Lisa and Jen have been helping her with her personal business and had told Rita that small things were happening like forgetting to clean after going to the bathroom and sometimes not remembering to pull off underpants before going. Theresa was also getting a bit more impatient and angry about common activities such as putting on socks that did not seem to be happening fast enough. Also, the childhood memories were becoming more frequent while yesterday's events were hardly ever recalled. Rita shed a few tears as she thought about this. They would have to do something very soon.

The one thing Rita and Theresa were able to talk about over the weekend was the money. They would give it to Father Hastings as they had planned. Neither one cared what others thought at this point. The cash had become a major point of contention between the people they loved. Rita was just shocked at what money could do to people and just wanted to get rid of it. Even Father Hastings had not been a model citizen during this drama, but they trusted that the money would be put to good use with him in charge. Given Theresa's situation, this needed to happen quickly. Rita doubted that Theresa would even remember this anymore although it seemed to have popped up at some inopportune times over the last few days, so who knew?

On Tuesday, around 10:00 a.m., the phone rang, so Rita answered.

"Hi, Aunt Rita, this is Paul."

"Oh, so glad you called, Pauly."

"Are you doing all right, do you need some help?"

"Lisa is here and Jen is coming later this afternoon, so we are all right." Rita got up and walked down the hallway. "Theresa is slipping fast, Paul. I don't think she remembers much of anything. She has been asking for Mom and has been forgetting to do everyday activities that used to be second nature."

Paul was sympathetic as the disease was progressing. "Oh, Aunt Rita, I'm sorry to hear that. Her disease must be advancing very fast. Do you need me home now?"

"No, we will be fine, just stop by on Thursday as you always do, and we can talk."

"Before I hang up, I just want to tell you a couple of things. Number one, I love both of you with all my heart. Secondly, I apologize for my actions regarding the money. I, along with you, wish I would never have seen it and wish it never existed. I have no objections to you giving this money to Father Hastings and the St. Joseph's Parish. I am here for both of you and will help you in any way possible. I don't need any money or repayment. Your conversation, beer, and coffee are more than enough for me."

"We love you too, Paul," said Rita. "I regret this money ever existed also as it led to some of the worst days of our lives over the last week. I'm glad you feel that way about this money as the only thing we want to do is get rid of it, so we will be calling Father Hastings today and would expect him to pick it up by tomorrow at the latest."

Paul thought to himself that it was a good thing he had let this go.

"That is fine, Aunt Rita. I am glad you are happy with your decision. I will be over on Thursday to put in the new furnace part and also to visit with both of you. I miss you and love you. Please call if you need anything else."

Jill had been eavesdropping and gave him a big hug. "It takes a big man to admit he was in error and apologize. A lot of people can't do that."

"Yes, I feel relieved but have one more call to make."

Paul dialed up Father Hastings once again, expecting the answering machine. He was surprised when the priest answered.

"Hello, Father Hastings? This is Paul Handelman. Please give me a minute of your time."

There was a slight pause. Then Father stated, "Sure, Paul, what's on your mind."

Paul had no intention of telling the priest about his aunt's wishes. He would find out soon enough.

"I would just like to say I am sorry for my actions on Sunday. While we may disagree on the money, I have made peace with the situation and have decided that whatever my aunts Theresa and Rita would like to do is their decision, and it will be just fine with me."

I'm glad that at least you have found peace, thought Father Hastings. "Apology accepted, Paul. I am also sorry it turned a bit contentious. I am pleased that the Lord has guided your actions. If we do receive the money, we will use it wisely."

Paul finished up. "They are two beautiful ladies, and all I want is to make sure they are safe and get what they need in their later years. Thank you for taking my call, Father."

Father Hastings closed by saying, "Thank you for calling. May the Lord bless you and your family, Paul."

Paul hung up the phone and asked Jill smilingly, "Who else did I piss off last week? Oh yes, the most beautiful person in the world. Since the weather is a little better today, should we at least ride to town for some lunch? I feel like a massive burden has been lifted. I don't know how some people can keep going through life lying, cheating, coveting, and accusing? How does their conscience deal with this? Do they think these actions are okay? I just hopped on that train for a few days, and I feel terrible for doing so."

Jill smiled. "You know how people are. If there isn't something in it for them, a lot of them simply don't care. There is a load of self-ishness, greed, and pettiness in the world today. A good friend is hard to find. I'm just happy to have a husband with a heart of gold. Yes, let's take a ride over to Two Harbors for some lunch."

Chapter 19

The rumor of the Handelman money was consuming the area as predicted by those who found out on Friday and Saturday. In addition to the passing of time, there are only a couple of events that could move a story of this magnitude to the background in a small town. Those would be a stronger rumor or a tragedy. Unfortunately, the area experienced the latter on Tuesday night.

Three Park Falls high school students were driving down County Highway E west of town when the driver lost control of the vehicle, went through a guardrail, and plunged twenty-five feet to the forest floor. Miraculously, the driver, Tom Peterson, managed to survive. His two passengers and best friends, Elliot Jansen and Shawn Stevens, were killed in the accident. Once Tom came to, he told a story of swerving to miss a deer in the road. According to the investigators, there was no reason to doubt Tom's version of the story.

As with any tragedy of this nature, the Jansen, Stevens, and Peterson families were devastated. However, in a smaller community, the grief does not only affect the immediate families but also consumes the whole town. Everyone knows most everyone else, and they feel the anguish nearly as strongly as the family members themselves. The outpouring of sympathy to these three families was nothing short of amazing with food, condolences, and heartfelt love being delivered for days. In the time of crisis, a small town always rallies around its own, and this was no exception.

The accident was now the front-page news and would drive the Handelman rumor to the background at least for the rest of the week. On Friday night at the high school football game, there would be a moment of silence for the boys. On Saturday, a joint memorial service at the Park Falls High School would be held for the public. Elliot and Shawn would be buried in private ceremonies the following week. As the Jansens were members of St. Joseph's Parish, Father Hastings was with the family for the better part of the week and worked with Lutheran pastor John Franklin, who knew the Stevens family, to plan the Saturday service.

Despite this added responsibility, the priest found time to drive over to Handelman Hill on Wednesday afternoon after receiving a call from Rita and Theresa on Tuesday. Father Hastings backed into the garage and closed the garage door behind him before knocking on the back entrance and letting himself in.

Father gave each of them a hug and sat down. "Are you sure this is what you want to do with this money?"

Rita replied, "Yes, please take it. The money has caused more problems than it is worth."

"Does everyone who knows about the money know I am getting it?"

"Paul knows and is fine with it," stated Rita. "Lindsey and Sheila are aware. We told them you would be getting it, but Lindsey is not happy. All the same, we told them, so please take this from us. When the time is right, please broadcast that this gift came from the Handelmans. That's all we ask. We don't mean to rush you, Father, but if you could move it to your truck and leave within thirty minutes, that wouldn't attract any attention. After that, Jen comes over to cook dinner."

Father Hastings responded, "Thank you so much. I have thought about it and will distribute it wisely to the parish, its members, and other worthy charities. The money is truly a gift that I could have never imagined. I will retrieve it and leave as you have requested."

The priest went downstairs with a hook tool and easily opened the magnet-lined door. There sat the eight suitcases. Just to be sure, he opened one of them to confirm the money was present. The suitcases were then carried to the garage two at a time and placed in the back of the Ford Explorer. As he grabbed the last two, he shined his flashlight around the room and determined it was empty. The priest then carefully closed the door, placed them in his vehicle, and covered everything with a blanket. He then stopped in the kitchen and gave Rita and Theresa a kiss and blessed them.

Father Hastings drove away as Rita closed the garage door behind him. With the money in the back of his SUV, he was very self-conscious of his driving and who might see him. The priest unexpectedly met a couple of cars on Old Horseshoe Road and was a little paranoid about who they were and what they might think. It was a very tense drive home as Father Hastings hoped he wouldn't get pulled over by the police or get in an accident. These types of things never happened to him, so he was unsure why this would be running through his head now but chalked it up to a long week.

The feelings did not stop when he arrived home. The priest backed into the garage, something he never did, and went into the house to try to figure out what to do with the money. Downstairs, spare rooms, closets, and just about every other room in the house was considered. Still, Father Hastings did not know what he wanted to do with this money. Besides himself and his guests, only his housekeeper visited, and that was just twice a week, so any of the storage options would work. Finally, he chose the spare bedroom closet.

Once again, Father Hastings hauled them two at a time to the spare bedroom. He then closed the curtains and shut the door before opening all the suitcases to check the contents. Everything was there. All four million dollars. He stacked them in the spare closet, covered them with a blanket, and piled up some shoes plus some miscellaneous items in front. Then Father retreated to the front room, turned on the television, and promptly began to worry about the money. To take his mind off this, he took a ride over to the Jansen residence to visit with the family.

At Handelman Hill, the mood was much different. Rita was relieved and pleased to be rid of the cash. She would deal with Lindsey later. Theresa in a moment of clarity asked if Father Hastings now had the money.

"Yes," said Rita. "Yes, he does. We no longer have to worry about this. I feel like a huge burden has been lifted."

Chapter 20

While Paul and Jill were vacationing in northern Minnesota, they had turned off the text notification on their phones. On the way back home Wednesday afternoon, they were flooded with text messages once they flipped it back on. Most of the news was about the horrific crash near Park Falls on Tuesday evening. While not close to any of the families involved, they did know them and were shocked to learn of this event. Jill called one of her friends to confirm the news. As part of the community, Paul and Jill would attend the football game on Friday night as well as the service on Saturday to offer their support to the families.

Thursday brought a return to sunshine for the area although the temperature was cooler at about fifty degrees. A perfect day to work outdoors, thought Paul. He cleaned up the leaves in his yard, ate lunch, and then drove out to visit his aunts.

"Hello, ladies," said Paul, smiling as he entered the kitchen. "How is everything? I need to install the new furnace ignitor, and then I'll clean up some more leaves in the yard if there is time."

"Oh, Paul, nice to see you. We are doing better," said Rita.

Theresa just sat in her chair looking at him and finally said, "Paul, yes, I remember you. Thanks for coming to visit."

Paul gave Rita a long look and saw the sadness on her face.

"Of course, Aunt Theresa, I love our visits! I'll be back upstairs for some coffee once I have fixed the furnace."

Paul marched downstairs with the part and his toolbox. After removing the old ignitor, his curiosity got the best of him, so he took a break from the repairs. He stepped back and looked at the safe, which was still partially open, probably meaning no one had been in it since him. Upon inspection, the same set of documents was in the same order. Believing no one else ever knew it was open, he closed and locked the safe. Then he used his hook tool to open the magnetic door and shined his flashlight around the hidden room. The suitcases were gone. A strange sensation came over Paul. A little bit of anger followed by an empty feeling of acceptance of the fact the money was not there and probably in Father Hastings' possession. He was not sure why, but he took one more look around with the flashlight, which confirmed the facts and carefully closed the door.

About fifteen minutes later, Paul had the ignitor installed and tested.

"Should be good to go for the winter," stated Paul as he entered the kitchen again.

Rita brought over a cup of coffee. "Thank you, Paul, you're the best! We don't know what we would do without you. Did you check to see if Father Hastings took all the money?"

"I did not," Paul lied. "But I assure you if you asked him to take it with him he did."

"I can't tell you how relieved we are," said Rita. "That money ate away at our father and was starting to do the same to us. Worse yet, it was affecting the people we love. Now it is in the hands of the church where it will do some good. Looking back, we should have given this cash away long ago."

Paul could not walk away from the subject and asked, "Now that the money is behind us, can you tell me more about it and how it affected my grandfather? You made several references over the last few days to this."

Theresa was napping in the living room, something that was occurring with much more frequency as the disease progressed, so Rita began. "Sure, we can talk now. Your grandfather received this money in 1988 after several years of fruitless pursuit of a mine. In my mind, the worst thing that happened to him was discovering gold in that test drill of his. He spent most of the 1980s trying to get permits, working on partnerships, and nothing panned out. The effort put into this took away from the time he spent in the family business, so Theresa and I ran it the last decade or so. By the time your grandfather received this offer, he was a tired and somewhat broken man. Robert Handelman did not miss the mark very often, and in his mind, this was a colossal failure."

Rita continued, "In reality, it was far from a failure and could have been deemed a success. Even the official sale of the Gogebic Range property netted a 25 percent profit. This figure doesn't count the four million dollars in cash. The funny thing is, your grandfather never made a deal like this in his life. He did everything by the rules, so this was a real contradiction for him. Theresa and I talked over the years, and we think maybe it was his way to get even so to speak, even though it doesn't seem to make much sense."

Paul responded, "Maybe he thought it was a payment for the time and energy he invested?"

"Something like that," said Rita. "He kept the money in the back corner of the basement for about a year but seemed nervous about it every day and checked it often. Finally, a local carpenter was hired to create the reinforced hidden space to store the money. Several times we asked him what he planned to do with it, and he never answered. I don't think he knew what to do. Your grandfather had become very possessive in his later years and had a hard time giving anything up. This is a huge amount of money, and eventually, we think, it wore him down to the point where he got very sick right before he passed away. Not a word was spoken about the money before he passed."

"Part of me wishes I hadn't asked," said Paul. "But thanks for sharing. It is very sad. Just think back on all the grief we went through over the last week due to this money. It sure affected all of us, and I also am glad it is not here anymore. Hopefully Father Hastings will be able to handle this gift better than we have."

Paul helped himself to another cup of coffee. Rita seemed relaxed enough when she talked about the money, so he doubled down. "Aunt Rita, I know it might be difficult for you, but can you tell me a little bit more about my father's relationship with my grandfather? I've always wondered about the thoughts they had about each other as it seemed less than family-like at times. You mentioned that

Dad and Grandpa reached a deal that gave him a loan and effectively severed all financial ties with him and the family."

"Sure, Paul," Rita began with a subdued voice. "Let me start by saying that Theresa and I loved your father. We envied him at times for his risk-taking and commitment to his passion. As you know, he absolutely loved cars and would do anything to be near them and work on them. I must say that he made the right choice and was a happy man, especially when he ran his own automotive shops in Green Bay. Theresa and I always wanted to be here. We loved the family business under Dad. Nothing could be better in our minds. It was truly an excellent life, but as we reflected back earlier this year, the what-ifs started to creep in as the family was the only life we have known.

"Theresa and I often wondered if we should have done something different or lived somewhere else? Would we have met a gentleman, married, and had children? What would Dad and Mom have thought? We were so tied up in the operations of the business and the family that we never really thought about it. It was probably a good thing we were there during the last decade of Dad's life as his focus was not where it should be most of the time."

The story was beginning to drift, so Paul tried to bring it back on track.

"Aunt Rita, what was the reaction when Dad decided to move to Green Bay? Do you know what caused him to leave the area and start fresh?"

Rita smiled. "Your father left because he was tired of being talked about. The Handelmans have always been very successful, and the rumors floated around back then just as they do now. The gossip circuit accused him of walking away from the family business, having a huge fight with his father, and just about every other thing imaginable. As a young man, this was too much to take, and Joe didn't care where he was as long as he had the opportunity to work on cars. Your grandfather collaborated with the local car dealer to line Joe up with a job in Green Bay. This showed his love for his son, but it also hurt him as he knew Joe would be living far away, and his hope for your dad ever joining the family business had passed.

"Your grandfather took this very hard. Theresa, Mom, and I talked to him and told him it was the best thing for Joe, but he just could not understand how his son could take a different path. Joe was the first to rebel, to use the term loosely, and Robert Handelman was not fond of this type of action, so the relationship was strained going forward. They did speak on occasion, and as you know, your father and mother would come to visit at least a couple of times a year. Your grandfather would stop in by Joe if he were down in Green Bay on occasion also, but he certainly didn't go out of his way to visit."

Paul asked, "Seems like my grandfather may have overreacted at times when things did not go his way. Was this the way he operated?"

"There was always a reaction, put it that way," said Rita. "He had a hard time letting go of anything and just could not understand when people did not want to do things his way or didn't listen to him. He ran the business with a great deal of control, which made it successful, but unfortunately, that power crept into his family life. Your grandfather was not an easy man to live with at times."

Rita continued, "That being said, he admired other successful people, and a part of him was very proud of your father's path. One day, Joe met with him and asked him for a loan so he could acquire two more shops in the Green Bay area. Your grandfather obliged, and you could see the pride on his face as he talked about his son. That pride also had a dark, sinister side, and he would not loan the money to Joe. Instead, he gave him the money on the condition that he signed off on any future money from the estate even in the event of your grandfather's death."

Paul needed to feign some surprise as he had already been through this a couple of days ago when he reviewed the papers.

"Dad actually signed off on this? Wow, this is kind of shocking. Of course, that would have given him the money he needed to be successful. I guess when you are in business, you take some chances."

Rita began again. "Yes, once he received this money, he was able to expand his business, and it was nice to see how well the two of you did together. This also seemed to lift a burden from Joe as he knew his position with your grandfather. It was just going to be one of those relationships that were not that close. As mentioned earlier, your grandfather just never let it go, and he insisted that we follow his instructions after he died. Your father was aware and was at peace with it, I believe. It really must have been hard on him though knowing that whatever he did, he could never really please his father."

"Yes, looking back it was hard for him," responded Paul. "He was a great man, and the thing is, he never acted that way with me. I had endless support, and he gave me more credit than he should have. He was truly an excellent father, friend, and business partner in my mind. I have learned maybe more than I wanted to about several things today, Aunt Rita, but thank you for taking the time to explain. Unfortunately, that's the way families work sometimes."

Paul concluded, "I can see Theresa is not doing as well as she was. Jill and I would like to take both of you out for dinner on Sunday afternoon if you wish. You can call Jen and tell her to take the night off. We'll pick you up around four and run out to The Settlement for some chicken. How does that sound?"

"Wonderful," said Rita. "I'll make sure Theresa takes a nap and will tell her we will go out to dinner. She will enjoy this also. Thank you, Paul!"

When Paul arrived home, he was feeling sentimental after all the talk about his father and grandfather. He went down to the basement and looked at the stack of cartons that contained some of his parents' belongings. These items had sat in containers for countless years. There were several dozen old country music cassette tapes that would never be played again. Paul wondered why it was so hard to part with stuff like this, but he knew the answer. This gave him a connection back to his parents, and it was good to view it now and then. He smiled through the tears as he went through some of the items before placing them back on the shelf.

Chapter 21

P rior to the start of the Friday night football game at Park Falls
High, a moment of silence was held for Elliot Jansen and Shawn
Stevens who had died earlier in the week in the tragic car accident.
Attendance was usually pretty good at these games, but this week it
was overflowing as the whole community showed up to support the
families of these young men. It seemed the only ones not in attendance and understandably so were Tom Peterson and his family. Tom
was injured very badly with a broken leg, ruptured spleen, and several broken ribs but was in stable condition and would survive. The
Petersons felt terrible not only for their son but also for the families
of Elliot and Shawn.

As always, only time can heal wounds this deep, but a small
community is also a forgiving one in cases such as this. Living in
northern Wisconsin buys you a lot of freedom and less to worry
about than the people living in large urban areas. However, it comes
with its own set of risks, one of which was driving on rural roads.
Swerving to miss a deer or other animal on the road was a common
occurrence. Sometimes, if you were lucky, you would just run into
the ditch, or you would hit the animal and not get hurt. Other times,
it ended in serious injury or tragedy. Tom was also mentioned during
the moment of silence, and prayers were offered up to the Petersons
as every parent in the crowd understood this could easily happen to
their son or daughter.

Saturday's service at the high school gymnasium was also well
attended. Jill and Paul filed in with the crowd and took a seat near
the back. Classmates put together several picture collages of the three

friends to share their memories along with a slideshow focusing mainly on the lives of Elliot and Shawn. The Lutheran pastor John Franklin started and talked about Shawn's life. Father Hastings did this same for Elliot. Both men were eloquent, sincere, and emphasized the importance of God in the boys' lives. Lastly, the high school principal, George Ambrose, said some kind words about all three students before asking for prayers and support for the families and others in need.

When the ceremony ended around 3:00 p.m., Jill and Paul were feeling sad for the families. Given their recent concerns, they hadn't thought much about this event until last night and today.

"Let's stop at Tony's for a beer," said Paul. "I can't imagine what those families are going through."

Jill agreed. "Yes, it is terribly tragic. The families must be devastated to lose those boys along with the hopes and dreams they had for the future. I could use a drink."

As Jill and Paul entered, the mood was somber at Tony's Bar as they were not the only ones who had come in from the memorial service. However, the big man still managed a smile and gave Jill a hug.

"Nice to see you again, Jill! Usually, the old guy just shows up alone."

They all laughed, which lightened the atmosphere a little.

"Nice to see you too, Tony! We were just at the memorial service. Just brutal when two excellent young men are involved in something like that," said Jill.

Tony replied, "I can only imagine. I snuck over to the game last night and was choked up by that. I don't know how well you know them, but these are three top-notch families. Each will have to deal with this incident in their own way for the rest of their lives. Events like this just rip a piece of your heart out, which can never be replaced. You sometimes wonder how many of these a person can take?"

Tony had been particularly insightful with this observation, thought Paul.

"Amen, well said. Things like this make you reflect on life and what is important, that is for sure." Tony walked off to serve other customers but returned after refilling their beers.

"By the way," said Paul, "thanks for calling the other day. I cannot begin to tell you everything that is going on at the Hill, but I thank you for looking out for me. Jill and I spent a few days up by Knife River, which allowed us, mainly me, to clear our heads."

Tony asked, "How are your aunts? Are they worried about the money?"

"Well, it appears they want to donate it to St. Joseph's church," stated Paul, lying a bit as the money had already been distributed. "They think Father Hastings should be in charge of this money so he could use it for charitable purposes."

Tony laughed. "Not sure how much you know about the good priest, but sometimes I hear he is not the most honest and trustworthy man in the world. I'm not sure if that is true or not as I do not know him. Just bar talk mainly."

"Well, I concur to a degree," said Paul. "I met with him last Sunday, and he got real defensive when I suggested he use it for various charities in the area, very unlike a priest. However, Jill and I came to the conclusion that the ladies can do what they wish with this money and hopefully soon. We are at peace with this. Have you heard any other rumors since we talked?"

"There is still some talk, but the events of this week drove it to the background," said Tony. "Still, there are a lot of people who know, and this is a pile of money, so I hope that Rita and Theresa are well protected. As tight as money is around here, I would make sure you have some protective security set up."

"I hear you," said Paul as he downed his beer. "Next week I plan to get some security cameras installed and have also told them to lock their doors and call me if there are issues. On top of this, Theresa's Alzheimer's disease is advancing, so we will be busy. Thanks for everything, brother! We will keep in touch."

Tony shook Paul's hand and wished both of them well.

Chapter 22

Sheriff John Bosworth pulled into work at the Price County Sheriff's Office located in the town of Phillips around 11:30 a.m. on Sunday. One of his deputies needed the afternoon off, so he was planning to cover his shift from the office until 5:00 p.m. The sheriff anticipated a slow day as it was Sunday and the Green Bay Packers were playing the Chicago Bears at noon. When the Packers are playing, most of Wisconsin is in front of a television set, which generally leads to three to four hours of relative peace for law enforcement officials throughout the state. John hoped to spend some time watching his favorite team in action himself between efforts to reduce his paperwork backlog.

Sheriff Bosworth started his career as a police officer in Minneapolis. The lure of action was attractive to young recruits, and during his three years working in the city, he had seen it all. The crime rate was astronomical in certain parts of the downtown area, and sometimes the best the police department could do was contain the violence to make sure it didn't spread to other parts of the city. Being a native of the Park Falls area, downtown Minneapolis was definitely on the opposite end of the spectrum regarding all aspects of life, legal and illegal.

After a couple of years, the prostitution, murder, drugs, and general decay of the human condition in the inner city began to wear on him. At first, he was astounded at how terrible one person could treat another. After seeing it for a prolonged period of time, he started to become numb to the violence which was a sign that he needed to get out. Longing for the beauty and serenity of the north woods, John was lucky enough to land a stint as a sheriff's deputy with Price County. Thirty years later, he sat in the sheriff's seat and was also reelected each time as his experience, fairness, and attitude were a hard combination to beat. Price County would someday get a new sheriff, but not until John Bosworth retired.

Probably more happened in a week in downtown Minneapolis than a year in Price County, but the last few days had been trying with the horrible car accident and death of the two young boys. This memory was still very fresh as he had been called out to help at the scene. Viewing the wreckage, it was truly a miracle that Tom Peterson survived. As he aged, these types of incidents bothered him more and brought on thoughts of retirement. Both John and his wife Angie were in good health now with Angie being a ten-year survivor of breast cancer. Maybe it was time to count their blessings and spend more time with family, friends, and each other.

As John entered, he greeted the jailer, Joe Berger.

"Morning, Joe, you and me today. Danny had to take the afternoon off, so I'll be working from the office."

"Oh, I see, send the boss in on Sunday to watch over me," Joe teased. "Nice to see you, John. I'll dial in the game soon. Big one today. They need to take care of the Bears."

The sheriff asked, "Do we have anyone in the overnight tank?"

"Just one. Our good friend Rollie McManus, caught sleeping behind the wheel at the stop sign last night in Phillips. Needless to say, he did not pass the sobriety test."

Sheriff Bosworth shook his head and replied, "For Christ's sake, how many damn DUI convictions does he have? Must be three or four. If they ever change the state laws, Rollie will be put away for a long time, and probably in prison. I'll go back and see how he's doing."

Upon entering the overnight holding area, he noticed Rollie sitting on the bench with his head down. The thing about Rollie was that he was a likable guy but just couldn't control the urge to get behind the wheel when he was drinking. It did not register with him that this was the wrong thing to do.

"Rollie, not again?"

Rollie replied, "I feel terrible, Sheriff. I don't know why I do this. I just tried to creep home from downtown."

The sheriff had heard this story many times before. "What if you would have hit someone walking on the road? This is dangerous behavior, Rollie. It would be great if you could work with the county to get some help. You are a good man, but in my opinion, the alcohol is interfering with your life."

"I know, Sheriff," repented Rollie. "Maybe it is time to get some help."

Sheriff Bosworth asked, "Do you have anyone to bail you out, or will you be spending the night?"

"You know that I can't come up with bail," said Rollie.

"Well, we'll see what we can do. I'll have Joe gather your belongings."

The Packer game had started, and Aaron Rodgers was well on his way to dismantling the Bears once again at Lambeau Field. It was shaping up to be a fine day in Packerland. Since Rollie was the only one incarcerated in the short-term hold, the sheriff released him and gave him a ride home at halftime. It did not make sense to the sheriff to keep a nonviolent detainee overnight, and Rollie's car was impounded so he wouldn't be tempted again. On the way home, Sheriff Bosworth stated the facts.

"Rollie, I'm giving you a break here by driving you home. In return, I want you to stay home the next few days, and you will also need to show up in court when ordered. If I hear that you are out around town, I will personally come and arrest you. It's ultimately up to you, my friend, but it would be advisable to seek some counseling, and don't even think about driving for a while."

Rollie knew he was lucky. "Yes, sir. Thank you, Sheriff."

The sheriff and the jailer settled in to watch the second half as the Green Bay Packers rolled the Chicago Bears 33–13. After the game had ended, Joe went to check on the other detainees, most of whom were in jail for domestic incidents or failure to pay money to those they owed. The sheriff started in on his paperwork. He texted his wife about 4:15 p.m. to say he would be home in about an hour and they could go out to dinner. Around four thirty, the phone in the sheriff's office rang after being routed in from the area 911 dis-patcher. John listened closely and slowly hung up. He then texted Angie to tell her something had come up and he didn't know when he would be home. Sheriff Bosworth grabbed his gear, let his dep-uties know of the situation, and sped down the road with his lights flashing and siren screaming.

Chapter 23

Like the rest of Packer Nation, Paul and Jill were also dialed into the Packer-Bear game and left the house with a smile around 3:45 p.m. to pick up Rita and Theresa for a little road trip to The Settlement to dine on some of their excellent fried chicken. When they pulled into the drive, they noticed the garage door was down, which was odd as the ladies usually had it open when they were expecting someone. Paul thought that maybe they were starting to take precautions, so he called Rita to announce their arrival. The phone rang about five times, and no answer was received.

Paul tried twice more and then began to worry. He had a key for the service door, so he entered and opened up the garage. When Jill and Paul entered the kitchen, Rita and Theresa were not there. Worse yet, there were signs of a struggle.

"Oh my god, Paul," shouted Jill. "Someone has broken in! There is some blood on the counter. Where are your aunts?"

Paul was also stunned but gathered his wits the best he could.

"Jill, settle down. We are going to have to look around the house from top to bottom to see if they are around. Dammit!"

They both took a couple of deep breaths and started the search upstairs. There didn't seem to be anything out of the ordinary up there. Then on the main level, everything was fine except in the kitchen. There were some bloodstains and a broken candleholder along with kitchen chairs scattered in disarray. Finally, Paul and Jill checked downstairs. The walls around the furnace looked to have been pounded on by a sledgehammer. Despite the beating, they were still intact. The safe also appeared to have been moved, but Paul suspected it was too heavy for the perpetrators to bother with. He gave Jill a look and went out to his truck to get the hook tool. When Paul pulled the door open, they didn't know what to expect and were very relieved to find it empty.

However, this did not help with the fact that his aunts were missing.

"One more thing, Jill," said Paul. "Let's take a quick look outside near the house." As they searched the perimeter of the estate home, it became evident that the ladies were not in the area or could not hear them. Paul screamed, "What in the hell happened!"

He dialed 911 and stated that he believed Rita and Theresa Handelman had been kidnapped. About twenty minutes later Sheriff Bosworth pulled up, followed closely by his two deputies, who began a search of their own on the premises while the sheriff talked to Paul and Jill.

Sheriff Bosworth started the questioning.

"Paul, are you sure that someone else didn't run by and pick them up today?"

Paul answered. "Not 100 percent sure, but we were scheduled to pick them up at four. If anything, my aunts like to be scheduled."

"Who do you think was the last person to see them today?"

"That would be Lisa Morris, their morning caregiver. Sheriff, I'm sure you have heard the rumors of the money over the last week or so."

"Yes, I have, do you have reason to believe this is a factor?"

"When Jill and I entered, there was a sign of a struggle in the kitchen, including chairs out of place, as well as some blood and broken candleholder. Also, in the basement, someone was smashing the wall with a sledgehammer, probably trying to find this money."

"This type of stuff just doesn't happen around here," stated the sheriff, thinking out loud. "Who in the hell would kidnap two elderly ladies? Do you think they got the money too?"

Part of Paul did not want to say, but given the circumstances, he had to confess his knowledge of the cash.

"John, the money was given to Father Hastings of St. Joseph's this week. It was not here. However, no one knows about this except me, my aunts, and Father Hastings. So that's why it appears on the surface that robbery of the cash may have been the motive."

The deputies returned and corroborated Paul and Jill's version and began the process of classifying the area as a crime scene. They would call in the local crime lab experts for DNA samples and photographs. More importantly, a silver alert would be issued for Rita and Theresa Handelman indicating they were missing.

Sheriff Bosworth rubbed his temples as a headache was brewing. With a crime of this magnitude, it wouldn't be long before the state authorities, and possibly the FBI, would be crawling up his ass. He followed protocol and called the Wisconsin State Crime Lab so they could assist the regional investigators in their efforts. It was getting dark very fast, so the deputies got their lights out and continued to search for the ladies around the perimeter and down by the river.

Once the silver alert hit local television and radio, the sheriff's office was flooded with calls to help locate the Handelman sisters. A group of local firefighters, EMTs, and people with law enforcement experience were asked to aid in the search that would continue throughout the night on and around the property. The last thing they needed was half of Price County trampling the potential crime scene, but it was imperative to keep looking as the temperature would be dipping near the thirty-degree mark. If Rita and Theresa were outside, there was a chance that they would not survive due to exposure.

After talking with Paul and Jill and receiving his deputies' report, Sheriff Bosworth concluded in his mind that the ladies were probably not around the property. The fact that the money was not found must have infuriated the perpetrators and most likely caused them to take Rita and Theresa with them to see if they could coax the location of the money out of them. When this thought hit him, he called Paul over.

"Paul, would you happen to know Father Hastings' phone number? Given the events of the day, he should probably be contacted and told to lock his house up and keep an eye on things."

"Yes, here it is," said Paul.

"I'll call him now," the sheriff stated as he dialed the phone. "You and Jill are welcome to stay for the search, or you are free to go.

Our plan for overnight will be to make sure we put our best efforts into combing the immediate area. The investigation will continue tomorrow. Thanks for all of your help, and my prayers are with both of you. Let's hope for the best."

"We will be staying to help," said Jill.

Father Hastings was informed of the situation and stated that he would lock his house and keep an eye out for anything out of the ordinary.

If the Handelman sisters were not located within the next couple of hours, this would become a statewide story and eventually would attract national media. To stay in front, Sheriff Bosworth placed a call to the county communications director, Connie Moore, who would set up a media center in Phillips for police briefings and any other news associated with this crime. Sheriff Bosworth would be controlling the information communicated, and Connie would be instructing the news organizations of the rules. Also, he had one of the state troopers cordon off the entrance to Old Horseshoe Road as well as the drive leading to Handelman Hill. Only residents with proof of identification and law enforcement personnel would be allowed through. No media allowed anywhere near at this time. It had been a long time since this part of the state had seen anything like this, but the sheriff knew it was best to prepare.

Through the use of volunteers and the help of a K-9 unit from the neighboring county, every square inch of the property was turned over by the time the sun was rising Monday morning. The conclusion the investigators came to was that the ladies were taken as far as the driveway, then probably loaded into a vehicle and taken away. While there was hope, the north woods were expansive and provided many options for those that were looking to hide anything. The body language of the volunteers who participated reflected this with the bowed heads and slumped shoulders. A difficult task lay ahead, and right now, no one knew the best way to continue.

Chapter 24

Around 7:00 a.m. Monday, Sheriff Bosworth thanked all the volunteers and called off the search, confirming the evidence led to the kidnapping of the Handelman sisters. He informed the volunteers that if the department needed further help, they might be contacted. Connie Moore called and stated that several local media outlets including television, radio, and newspaper personnel were waiting at the office for an update. The sheriff drove over to give them the latest news and coordinate the day's efforts before he went home to get some sleep.

"Ladies and gentlemen," started Sheriff Bosworth. "First of all, thank you for respecting our wishes and reporting to the media center. Around four thirty yesterday afternoon, the sheriff's department received a call of a possible kidnapping on Old Horseshoe Road at the home of Rita and Theresa Handelman. Their nephew, Paul Handelman, and his wife, Jill, were scheduled to pick them up around 4:00 p.m., and when they entered the home, the ladies could not be found.

"The area is still an active crime scene under investigation, so I won't take any questions. I can tell you that a group of volunteers including local firefighters, EMTs, and law enforcement officials along with a K-9 unit spent the night searching the property. The conclusion we reached this morning is that Rita and Theresa Handelman had been taken from the property. As you know, a silver alert was issued, and I ask you to get your message out in case anyone has seen Rita or Theresa since yesterday. Investigative work will continue around the clock, and Connie will let you know when the next update will be. Thank you."

The sheriff then met with state and local authorities to map out the plan for the day. The first order of business was that anyone who had participated in the overnight search would need to go home and get some sleep. During his time at Handelman Hill, the sheriff had worked closely with Paul to gather together a list of people to talk to regarding their whereabouts on the day of the incident and anything else they might know. This group included caregivers Lisa Morris and Jen Matthews. Also, Lindsey Barrington, Sheila Nackers, and finally Father Hastings. These people along with Paul and Jill formed the Handelman Hill inner circle. Detective Bill Allen of the Wisconsin Division of Criminal Investigation would be conducting these interviews. The FBI had been informed and would be involved to some extent very soon.

Jen Matthews was the first to arrive at 12:00 p.m. in Phillips to interview with the detective. Each person was informed that the interview would be taped.

"Hi, Jennifer," began Detective Allen, "can you tell me your relationship to Rita and Theresa Handelman?"

"Please call me Jen. I am their evening caregiver. I come over in the evening to cook dinner for the sisters and make sure everything is in order before they go to bed. You probably know this, but there is another morning caregiver also." Jen was getting choked up. "Detective Allen, why would anyone do this? These ladies are the sweetest in the world."

"That's what we are trying to find out, Jen. Were you scheduled to come over Sunday evening?"

"No, Rita called and told me to take the night off as Paul Handelman, their nephew, and his wife, Jill, were picking them up to go to dinner. Usually, I would be there, but not that night."

"Can you tell me what you were doing between 12:00 p.m. and 4:00 p.m. Sunday afternoon?"

"Yes, I went to the grocery store, then over to my mom and dad's house to watch the Packer game and have dinner. Did you need their names?"

Having conducted his share of witness interviews, the detective had a good read on people and was pretty sure Jen was not involved.

"No, not right now, Jen. We'll contact you again if we need that. Do you have anything else you would wish to offer that may help in our investigation?"

"Just the fact that almost the entire town heard a rumor that there was money at the estate. Every once in a while, I would hear Rita and Theresa talking about this, but didn't pay much attention. My job was to make dinner and take care of them while I was there. In return, they took good care of me. It's just that a lot of people heard the money was there, so there is no telling who may have done this."

"Thank you, Jen. We will contact you if we need further information."

Lisa Morris was next, and the testimony was almost identical. She also had a good alibi and expressed some emotion as they talked about the situation. The detective asked her one additional question. "When you left at noon, what state was the house in. Were doors locked or open?"

"I left the garage door on the left side open as Rita had instructed. Paul and Jill were coming over around four, and the ladies were going to take a nap, so she decided to leave it open for him at that time. I did not see anything unusual when I left. Earlier in the week, there was a lot of traffic, but that calmed down. I did not meet one car on Old Horseshoe Road, very quiet."

Around 2:00 p.m., Father Hastings showed up for his interview.

"Good afternoon, Father, thank you for coming by," started Detective Allen. "I understand you have received a lot of money from the Handelman sisters. Where do you have this money right now?"

"It is at home presently. I just picked it up the other day. It will be used by the church to help our people and also to help other charities in the area."

Not being familiar himself, the detective still asked the question. "Are you familiar with the laws and regulations regarding the transfer and use of this amount of money?"

"Oh yes," lied the priest rather nervously. "We will be taking care of that in the next few weeks. Everything needs to be legal before we would distribute."

"Does this money make you nervous?"

"Yes, it does, especially after what happened to Rita and Theresa. The sheriff informed me of this last night and asked me to take precautions."

"Can you tell me where you were between 12:00 p.m. and 4:00 p.m. on Sunday?"

"Yes, I went out to lunch and then visited some shut-in members of our parish. I then returned home to watch the end of the Packer game and remained home. I got the call from the sheriff early evening."

"All right, thanks for your time, Father. If you see or hear anything, please let us know."

"I will do that and will pray for Rita and Theresa."

Detective Allen received the same vibe others did when they talked to Father Hastings. On the surface, things appeared normal, but there seemed to be something about him that made you question his honesty and integrity. Bill was not sure what this was, but he had the feeling, which didn't make much sense as the money was already in his hands, so he would have no reason to kidnap the Handelman sisters. But like a good detective, he made a note of it.

At 3:00 p.m., Lindsey Barrington arrived to talk to Detective Allen who began, "Can you tell me about your relationship with Rita and Theresa Handelman?"

Lindsey put on as much charm as was possible. "Yes, I am their legal counsel. I have been for well over two decades and know the ladies like relatives. I was shocked to hear this news last night."

"What did you know about the money?"

Lindsey played it close to the cuff. "I've heard some rumors of the money and that there was probably a lot of cash on the property, but I have never seen this money."

"Can you tell me where you were between the hours of 12:00 p.m. and 4:00 p.m. on Sunday?"

"Yes, I was at a friend's house watching the Packer game. Did you need his name?"

"Not right now. Is there anything else you could tell me that may help us find Rita and Theresa?

"I can't think of anything right now. I feel terrible that this happened as I just visited them last weekend. If I hear something, I will let you know."

"Thank you, Ms. Barrington."

Bill Allen had interviewed lawyers before, and this was fairly typical. Answer the question with the least amount of detail possible. However, if the alibi checked out, there was no reason to suspect Lindsey of anything at this time.

Sheila Nackers was next. As she entered the room, her eyes were very puffy from crying.

"Are you all right, Ms. Nackers?"

"Excuse me, Detective Allen, but this has not been easy on me. I consider myself a good friend of Theresa and Rita as I have handled their financial affairs for decades. Lindsey Barrington and I visit them often to talk about legal and monetary concerns."

"Are you good friends with Lindsey Barrington?"

Sheila was an open book today. "Yes, we are friends but are very different in a lot of ways. I have a personal interest in the ladies whereas I think, sometimes, my friend is more interested in money although she does provide legal counsel when needed. The Handelman sisters are almost like family. Lindsey and I are in their will as we have been taking care of their affairs for decades."

Detective Allen tried to keep his game face on. "Can you tell me what you know about the money?

"Well, as you have probably heard through the rumor mill, there is a lot of cash. I have no idea where it is, and I have no interest in it. The last I heard, the ladies were going to give this to Father Hastings and the St. Joseph's Parish. Do you think this is why Rita and Theresa were kidnapped?"

"I can't answer that, Ms. Nackers. Can you tell me where you were between the hours of 12:00 p.m. and 4:00 p.m. on Sunday?"

"Yes, I was visiting my daughter and her family. I arrived back home around three thirty."

"Thank you, Ms. Nackers. If you hear anything, please let us know."

Detective Allen had completed his first round of interviews, and it appeared three out of the five were genuinely concerned about the Handelman sisters and were very broken up. The lawyer and priest were hard reads although he seriously doubted either one was involved. The whole area knew, so there were literally thousands of potential suspects. Paul Handelman was stopping by later this evening to give an official statement, so he would ask him for his take on the five folks that he just interviewed.

Chapter 25

Connie Moore had scheduled the next press conference for 6:00 p.m. By now there had been mention of this on several national news channels, and the makeshift press room was jammed to capacity. Sheriff Bosworth arrived about 5:30 p.m. after a restless daytime sleep but looked much fresher than he had in the morning. Crime lab work was still in progress at Handelman Hill as were the interviews with those who knew Rita and Theresa Handelman.

"Ladies and gentleman, thank you for your patience," Sheriff Bosworth began. "Unfortunately, we do not have much new to report. The crime scene investigation continues as do the interviews with close family and friends. There have been some reports regarding the silver alert that turned out to be false. As this point, we do not know the whereabouts of Rita and Theresa Handelman.

"Once again, I will not take questions at this juncture. The FBI has sent an agent up to assist, so we will work with the State and the FBI to develop a plan going forward to find these folks. We ask that you refer any leads to our office, and please respect the privacy of the Handelman family and others that are closely involved. Connie will send out notification of the next briefing. It will be sometime tomorrow. Thank you."

The press corps was not happy with this having waited most of the day. Sheriff Bosworth didn't care as there were two missing people to find. He left the press area and headed to a conference room in the back. Waiting for him were Detective Allen and Agent Tom Macklin from the FBI. Macklin was sent up from Chicago as he had a lot of experience in kidnapping cases. Sheriff Bosworth briefed both men in detail on the events up to this evening.

Agent Macklin asked, "Have there been any demands for ransom or the delivery of this money?"

"Oddly no," stated the sheriff. "We think the perpetrators may be trying to find out exactly where this money is as they did not find it at the house. I hate to think what they may be doing to the sisters."

"Yes, that is odd," answered Agent Macklin. "In my experience, these folks are not especially patient and usually will release their demands very early. However, not finding the cash at the house may have led to an impromptu kidnapping. Maybe that was not part of the plan until there was no money."

Sheriff Bosworth responded, "All I know is that this is some big wilderness up here, and they could be keeping these ladies damned near anywhere. It is also cold at night, and I worry about their survival. Short of searching every building within a few miles, I'm not sure what we can do? The state and local authorities stopped at all residences on Old Horseshoe Road today to see if anyone saw anything suspicious. Outside of a lot of cars early in the week when the rumor broke, they came up empty. Bill, how did the interviews go with the friends of the family?"

Detective Allen recapped the five interviews with the initial judgment that he believed all had an alibi. They discussed Lindsey Barrington and Father Hastings for a bit although they agreed that it would have been more suspicious if all five had behaved in the same way. There was no reason to suspect any of them at this point.

Agent Macklin summarized, "With the word of the money spreading the way it did, just about everyone in the county is a suspect. I don't have an answer on how to proceed at present except to keep collecting and sorting information as it comes in. Continue to interview people close to the family. Have local police put out some feelers to restaurant, tavern, and other business owners to keep their eyes and ears open for any activity out of the norm. Small-town gossip can also work in your favor if something leaks out inadvertently. Right now, we do not have enough evidence to look at phone records and such. Secrets like this sometimes are buried forever, but more times than not, they surface due to human error and God's good grace. It looks hopeless now but keep turning over the rocks and let's see what we come up with. Great job to this point, gentlemen."

Sheriff Bosworth was impressed so far by the FBI agent. A lot of times the agency would send up a real dickhead who wanted to take over the investigation and viewed local authorities as peons who just got in the way. Agent Macklin appeared very fair and cooperative. Lord knows, they needed all the cooperation they could get.

About 7:15 p.m., Paul Handelman entered the law enforcement building in Phillips and asked for Sheriff Bosworth. He was guided back to the conference room where all three men were waiting.

Paul raised his eyebrows upon entering, and Sheriff Bosworth spoke, "Hi, Paul, thanks for coming down. I would like to introduce you to Detective Bill Allen from the State of Wisconsin and FBI agent Tom Macklin who has a lot of experience in these types of cases. Our original plan was an official statement from you, but if you didn't mind, I would like these two gentlemen to listen in."

Paul shook hands with both men. "No problem, I wasn't expecting this, but it makes sense as they are here to help."

Paul gave his official version to the three, which included a narrative on how he discovered the money and who knew what about it at this point. Detective Allen then asked Paul his thoughts about the five people he interviewed that afternoon and if he thought they might be involved.

"Let's start with Jen Matthews."

"Rita and Theresa loved Jen. She was their nighttime caregiver cooking dinner and making sure everything was in order before they went to bed. Theresa has Alzheimer's disease that is progressing fast, so Jen's patient and loving care was valued greatly by my aunts. No way she would ever be involved in something like this."

"How about Lisa Morris?"

"Ditto what I said about Jen. Fantastic caregiver and no way she would be involved. These two are angels on earth."

"Father Hastings?"

A slight pause on Paul's part. "Well, I had a meeting with the good priest about a week ago and told him I was not very happy my aunts were giving all this money to him. He told me to look to the Lord for guidance, and it was my aunt's decision. I did come to peace with it, thankfully, as Rita and Theresa gave him the money just this week. There's something about him that I don't trust, but I have talked to him and told him that I was all right with the decision, and we are now on good terms. Given the fact he already has the money, it wouldn't make sense for Father Hastings to be involved."

"How about Lindsey Barrington?"

"She is part of the financial and legal duo along with Sheila Nackers that manage my aunt's affairs. I do not know them all that well, but they seem like the odd couple. They have been working with my aunts for decades and have ended up in their final will for about 95 percent of the assets. My aunts had an argument with Lindsey just last week over the cash as she confronted them wondering where this money was. I don't believe they have been in contact since, and Lindsey does not know Father Hastings now has this money. Knowing what I know, she could most definitely be a suspect as she was looking for this money a week ago."

"Sheila Nackers?"

"Seems like she was the voice of reason within the odd couple. However, I do not know her that well, and she is part of my aunts' final will. She doesn't seem like the type to be involved in something like this, but if Lindsey was involved, she might be."

Detective Allen stated, "Paul, thanks for your candor and your observations. We are still working diligently and will be in touch if something comes up. Our prayers are with you."

When Paul left the room, the three men rehashed the events of the day.

Detective Allen began, "Paul's observations go hand in hand with mine including his feelings on Father Hastings and Lindsey Barrington. However, it is not unusual to have contrasts when interviewing people about events of this nature. Right now, all of them appear to have an airtight alibi. Lindsey is an interesting case though. She wanted that money badly according to Paul."

Agent Macklin was next. "Yes, it was interesting, but as you say, Detective, contrasts exist, and we need to stay focused on the evidence. Paul Handelman was taken to the cleaners by his own family here the way it sounds, yet he is at peace with it. He is either an exceptional man or is hiding something."

Sheriff Bosworth stepped in. "If he were acting, he would have won an Oscar. I was there with him from the onset, and his concern for his aunts is genuine. Paul is a good man who was put through an awful two-week period here. He is financially secure and would not need any of this money. His heart is with his aunts. However, it's no surprise that he expressed some bitterness at the fact that Lindsey and Sheila are primaries in the Handelman sisters' will."

With that, the three left the room with more information but still nothing to go on. The situation looked quite hopeless right now, but the teams would continue to gather data and move forward from there. This crime happened during the Packer-Bear game, so the chance of finding any eyewitnesses was slim. A nuclear bomb could go off in Wisconsin during a Green Bay Packers game, and half the folks wouldn't notice.

In the meantime, the media had time to kill and not a lot of information, so they filtered out through Phillips and into Park Falls and began conducting some "man on the street" interviews to determine what the locals were thinking. Most of the interviews ran similar to the one that ABC News delivered when they ran into Scooter Kosloski as he was walking from one watering hole to another: "It's been known that the Handelmans had a lot of money buried up there, and I think someone has finally found it. I just hope they don't hurt the ladies." Everyone seemed to have a different opinion regarding the money, but all were very concerned for Rita and Theresa Handelman.

Chapter 26

Park Falls police officer Jordan Pearce was in his patrol car just off Highway 13 on the north end of town Tuesday morning where the speed limit drops from fifty-five miles per hour down to thirty watching for those going a little too fast. Even though there was police presence several times a week, the action was plentiful. So far today, two warnings and one speeding ticket were written. About 9:00 a.m., Officer Pierce received a radio call to respond to a break-in at the residence of Father Hastings near St. Joseph's Catholic Church. He turned his flashing lights on and pulled into the driveway about ten minutes later.

Upon entering the home, he found housekeeper Irene Nelson in a full panic.

"Oh, my god, Officer! I arrived to clean this morning and found this! I don't know what to do? Father Hastings seems to be severely injured!"

The first thing Officer Pearce did was check on the priest and saw a pretty good-sized lump on his head but no bleeding.

"Father, can you see me and understand me?"

"Yes, I am coming to, but my head still hurts. My memory is foggy right now, but I know that someone hit me over the head sometime last night."

"I will call an ambulance to get you checked out. You may have a concussion."

Father Hastings did not argue.

Next, the officer looked around the house, which appeared to have been ransacked. Having knowledge of the events from Sunday, the best thing to do in his mind was to put in a call to his boss. Park Falls police chief Ed Collins was not on duty but arrived soon after in street clothes, looked around, and waved Officer Pearce into the garage area.

"Jesus Christ, our worst fear. Father Hastings was in possession of the money, so I would guess it is no longer here. I'll call Bosworth and make sure his team gets up here as soon as possible. Let's make sure everything stays the way it is. Keep an eye on the housekeeper so she doesn't touch anything. I'm sure the investigators will want to interview her, so take her to a spot away from most of the commotion and ask her to stay."

The Park Falls EMTs pulled up in the ambulance and entered the home to find Father Hastings lying on the couch with his head propped up.

"How do you feel, Father Hastings, are you experiencing lightheadedness?"

"A little less right now. Just my head hurts where I was hit."

One of the EMTs did a check around the neck and shoulder area and determined that everything was intact enough for a trip to the hospital, so Father Hastings was loaded on a gurney and transported.

Officer Pearce approached Irene Nelson. "Ms. Nelson, why don't you come into the kitchen area toward the back door. We would like you to stay a little while until the investigators get here."

Irene was still shocked. "Are they investigating the break-in? I don't know what these people would take from Father Hastings as he is just a priest, but they sure turned the house upside down. It will take awhile to tidy it back up for him."

The officer was privy to the fact that Father Hastings had the money, but most others did not know, and it was evident that Irene was in this latter category.

"I'm not sure, but that's what we will try to find out. We'll have to leave everything as it is now until the investigators are through with their work."

Sheriff Bosworth pulled up to the house, followed closely by FBI agent Macklin and Detective Allen. He met Chief Collins outside the garage, lit up a Marlboro, and took a deep drag.

"Still puffing those heaters, John?

"Maybe in my next life I'll have some fucking willpower. What the Christ is going on around here, Ed?"

"Not good, John, we left the scene as is and just concentrated on getting Father Hastings to the hospital as he had a possible concussion. The house is turned upside down. Since he had the money here, I would guess it is probably missing but don't know for sure. His housekeeper, Irene Nelson, reported this as she walked in on it about eight forty-five this morning. She is still very shaken up."

"You know, Angie and I were just thinking of retirement soon, but that sure as hell won't be happening at least until this blows over. We have two missing people, a priest that has been victimized, and probably some missing money. Now we will be fighting this on two fronts."

"I hear you. If Park Falls PD can help in any way, let us know. Otherwise, we'll get out of your way."

"Thanks, Ed, what I would ask is that you work with my office and make sure this house is watched 24/7 until the agencies have what they need."

Officer Pearce and Chief Collins drove back to the police station to formulate their plan.

After a quick glance and conversation with Agent Macklin, Detective Allen called in some state and local criminal investigators as the house was a mess and it would need to be picked through very carefully to determine if the money was stolen and also to collect any evidence that might have been left behind. It was imperative that they find out where Father Hastings kept this money to start with, so the first thing he did was ride up to the hospital.

Detective Allen started, "Father Hastings, how are you feeling?"

"Less dizzy but getting a little headache. I believe I was hit over the head by someone."

"We will let you rest today and will visit tonight with a few questions if you are feeling well enough. In the meantime, we need to know one thing. Where did you keep the four million dollars you received?"

Father Hastings was a little hesitant as if he was still protecting it but finally stated, "In the spare bedroom closet. I should have put it somewhere safer but just received it."

Detective Allen put his hand on the priest's shoulder. "That is all we need to know for now, Father, please get some rest."

Detective Allen called the sheriff and relayed the news. The investigators had just arrived and were formulating their plan. Based on the information received, one of them carefully tiptoed into the spare bedroom and checked the closet. There were clothes and other articles scattered, but no suitcases of cash.

"Not a surprise," said Sheriff Bosworth, "but keep it here for now until we know for sure."

Chapter 27

B ack at Handelman Hill, the state and local investigation teams were finishing up searching and collecting evidence. The only problem is that it would be a few weeks before they could obtain the DNA test results, and this would just be against a known database of people with criminal convictions. Regardless, the state crime lab needed to collect and catalog all evidence and have it ready in case a suspect was arrested.

The investigators informed the state and the FBI that there was not a lot left behind by the perpetrators. There were a few fingerprints lifted, some hair, and of course, the blood, but this could be directly related to Rita and Theresa. No one knew at this point. The police blockade of Old Horseshoe Road and the entrance to the home was taken down. For the next week or so, the Price County sheriff's department would have a deputy posted at the site in case someone tried to return to the scene of the crime. Paul and Jill Handelman were granted permission to visit Handelman Hill with the advice to lock it up tight and to set up a security system with cameras as soon as they had the opportunity.

The couple was extremely worried about Rita and Theresa as it had been two days since they were last seen and law enforcement did not seem to be any closer to a resolution. They drove over to Handelman Hill and walked through the home one more time to determine if any action was needed. Outside of a little bit of tidying up, the condition of the interior was back to normal.

Jill stated, "Paul, now that we are done cleaning, can we please leave? It is just creepy without your aunts here."

Paul patted Jill on the shoulder. "Yes, we can go. There is nothing else we can do at this time, and I agree with you that it is empty and strange right now. I'll let the deputy know that I will come back later by myself to pick up some of the leaves in the yard for the last time. Also, I'll contact some security firms and get some estimates. I can't tell you how low I feel. This is awful."

At Father Hastings' residence, Detective Allen began a conversation with the housekeeper.

"Ms. Nelson, what time did you arrive, and what did you see when you first walked in?"

"I let myself through the back door at about eight forty-five this morning as I do twice a week. I noticed right away that some items were scattered in the kitchen." At this point, Irene began to cry a bit. "Father Hastings, he, he was lying on the couch holding his head. I did not know if he was even alive. The living room was in shambles with pictures knocked over along with some furniture. I talked to Father, and he was very groggy, groaning as he moved, but he was starting to talk. I was worried mainly about him at this point, so I called 911 and did not look any further. Is he going to be all right?"

"The report I received from the hospital is that he will be okay. He may have suffered a concussion but will recover. You said he was starting to talk, do you remember what he said?"

"He just kind of mumbled about someone hitting him over the head. I didn't get anything more out of him except that the people who did this left."

"There was more than one?"

"He said 'they' left so I would assume so. That's all I have."

"Thanks, Ms. Nelson. The residence will be cordoned off as a crime scene, and the investigative team will be gathering evidence for some time. We will inform you when we are through, and at that time, you may return."

Once again, the state and local crime scene investigators went to work. This looked like a garbage dump compared to what they encountered on Handelman Hill, so the process would certainly take a lot longer as they needed to go through one step at a time. By the time evening had arrived, the preliminary work had determined that there was no money on site. It had been stolen.

Detective Allen and Agent Macklin received permission from the doctor on duty, so they drove over to the hospital for a visit with Father Hastings.

"Father Hastings, how are you feeling this evening?"

"A little better, I still have a headache, but other than that I am recovering."

"Can you tell us about the events of last night and this morning?"

"Sure, I can remember most of it. Last night around nine thirty my doorbell rang. When I opened the door, two men with hoods pulled over their face forced their way past me and into the house. They asked where the money was. How they knew about it, I don't know."

"Please continue."

"I denied it and asked them what they were talking about. That's when the bigger one hit me over the back of the head with something that was hard. I lost consciousness for a while. When I woke up, I was alone on the couch with the lights off in the house. I looked at the clock, and it was 4:30 a.m., and my head was pounding. I tried to get off the couch but could not. Apparently, I fell back asleep and was discovered by Irene this morning."

"Did you look around the house at all when you awoke the first time?"

"No, I was still out of it at that point, so I had no idea what had occurred. I am guessing the money is gone?"

"The crime scene is still being investigated. Can you tell us any more about the two men who entered your home?"

"One was a larger man, over six feet tall, the other average height. The smaller one did the talking although I did not recognize the voice. I did not see any features as they were covered from head to toe."

"Can you tell us why you would have opened the door without checking who it was? Especially after being given the warning?"

"Nothing other than habit. I am a Catholic priest and have helped distressed parishioners and others at any time of the day or night for my whole life. My door is always open. That is why it was a big mistake on my part to keep the money there. I am a person who helps others in need, but looking back, I should have exercised more caution and will do so going forward."

"Thank you, Father. Just so you know, evidence will be gathered from your home for quite a few days, so when you are discharged, you will need to report to the Park Falls police station. The officers there will give you some of your clothes, your vehicle, and an allowance to stay at a local motel for a few nights. A law enforcement official will be available to stay with you if you desire."

Before they left the hospital, Agent Macklin and Detective Allen met with Dr. Anjani, who was on duty when Father Hastings arrived at the hospital.

"Doctor, thanks for taking some time to talk to us. There was a crime committed at Father Hastings' residence, and we need to get some information from you. Can you describe how Father Hastings was when he arrived via ambulance and what you found?"

"Sure, when he arrived, I did an initial check and then received an update from the EMTs. The only injury that he had was decent-sized bump to the head. I have no doubt that he would have a headache, but it did not look too severe as there was no bleeding or severe contusions. On the other hand, head injuries are tricky, especially when people are older, so we treated it as a possible concussion. We performed a CAT scan and found nothing abnormal. Father Hastings passed the concussion protocol this evening, and I am recommending he be released tomorrow."

"Would this type of injury be consistent with getting hit over the head with an object?"

"Yes, it could have been caused by this. If you ever bumped your head on a doorjamb or wall by accident and it knocked you back for a bit, this is what it looked like to me. It hurts at the time but usually goes away in a day or two."

"Do you think Father Hastings would have lost consciousness for a while with an injury like this."

"He could have, but I don't believe it would have been for long. However, as I mentioned earlier, head injuries affect people differently, and he could have been out for a while. On the plus side, we'll give him a couple more tests, but I believe he will be good to go tomorrow."

"Thanks, Dr. Anjani. We'll let you know if we have any other questions."

Chapter 28

S heriff Bosworth had returned to headquarters earlier Tuesday afternoon to process all the events of the day. Connie Moore had scheduled the daily press briefing for 8:00 p.m., so he needed to take some time to frame up the information to make it acceptable to the media. The sheriff knew they were pissed off regarding yesterday's briefing, so he wanted to make this one better and also try to have the media work with them instead of being adversarial. That would be the challenge.

Around four that afternoon, he received a call.

"Hi, Sheriff, this is Amy Sutherland. I work at Dansby Manufacturing in Park Falls and have some information to pass on to you that may help."

Sheriff Bosworth had received quite a few calls of this nature that proved to be worthless, but they were at a dead end, so he was listening.

"Hi, Amy, thank you for calling. What type of information do you have?"

"Well, there is this guy at work, Carl Hanson, that did not show up on Monday. When he came in today, he had a cut above his eye that didn't look like it was attended to very well. He is a little odd but usually somewhat talkative. Today he was not and was very quiet and reserved."

The sheriff asked, "Do you think maybe he got into a fight with his relatives or something like that? That could cause a man to be humbled as you stated." Unfortunately, these types of incidents were way too common in the north woods as were the self-healing methods practiced by some folks as they just did not want to go to a doctor.

"Carl isn't like that. He isn't married and is not a fighter that I know of. Maybe it is nothing, but I thought I would let you know as he was off on Monday and showed up today looking roughed up and was not acting as he normally does."

"Amy, thank you for calling in and let us know if this behavior continues after a day or two."

Sheriff Bosworth called one of his deputies into the room to run a background check on Carl Hanson. The data showed a run-in with the law ten years prior regarding shooting deer out of season. He was fined several thousand dollars and had his hunting license revoked for life. While this was more a Department of Natural Resources issue, it was a criminal conviction and showed that Carl was caught bending the law at one point in his life. He would let Allen and Macklin make the call on this one. They did have a broken candleholder and blood in the kitchen as evidence, so it was intriguing.

Around 7:00 p.m., Detective Allen and Agent Macklin returned to headquarters. The town and surrounding area were buzzing like a hornet's nest as word had spread regarding Father Hastings. The first order of business was to discuss what information to release at the press conference. There might be a benefit to discussing the Father Hastings robbery in detail, but they decided against it as only law enforcement and a few people knew he had the money in the first place. It might cause more harm than good if these two events were unrelated. Also, the three agreed this was probably too much for the town to absorb at this point. The press would hate it, but the conference would again be rather vague, mentioning the incident but treating it as unrelated.

At 8:00 p.m., Sheriff Bosworth addressed the packed press room.

"Good evening, ladies and gentlemen, and thanks for waiting all day. Because of the sensitive nature of the investigation, once again I will not take questions. Today the Wisconsin Department of Criminal Investigation wrapped up its work at the Handelman residence. All evidence has been gathered and is being cataloged. As mentioned earlier, at this point, we believe Rita and Theresa Handelman have been kidnapped. We continue to receive leads and information but right now have not come up with anything actionable.

"As I'm sure you have heard, earlier today, Father Hastings' residence was broken into in Park Falls. Father was hurt during the encounter and is currently in the hospital with non-life-threatening injuries. Our office will be looking into this crime also, but the majority of our efforts will continue to be on locating Rita and Theresa Handelman.

"Members of the media, I thank you for being patient and cooperating with our mandates. As is the nature of any active criminal investigation, the content of information that I pass on to needs to be limited. The crimes that were committed the last couple of days are very rare in northern Wisconsin, but with the help of local, state, and federal experts, we are executing a plan and moving forward as urgently and prudently as we can. Remember, it has been just over forty-eight hours since the initial call regarding the Handelmans. We ask that you report anything you may hear to the sheriff's office. News conferences will be suspended until we have something new to pass along. Once again, thank you for your patience."

The grumble from the press corps was a little more subdued this time as they understood the consequences. However, news had a short cycle, and forty-eight hours in this world was a lifetime, leading most of the national media outlets to pull out. There were bigger stories in the nation and world to address, so their local affiliates could cover this story if anything broke.

Connie Moore entered the conference room in the back.

"Sheriff Bosworth, you should be a politician someday. Great job with the media. I believe we will just be working with local outlets from here on in. Overall, they were not happy, but they understand there is not much more that we can report at this point."

"Thank you, Connie," stated the sheriff. "I'm sure glad we got out in front of the events especially given the developments of today. This could have blown sky-high without organization and controlled information release. I would guess that very soon we will have something to report, and I will update you when that happens. We need to prepare as the rumor mill is swirling with these two crimes, but we have bought a little time."

Detective Allen, Sheriff Bosworth, and Agent Macklin exchanged stories from their long day. They were all intrigued by the interviews with Father Hastings and Dr. Anjani. It was hard to say, but maybe the priest was overreacting to the bump on his head for some reason. If a person is knocked out most of the night, you would expect the physical damage to be more severe, but as the doctor stated, people react to head injuries differently. Macklin and Allen were unquestionably interested in the story of Carl Hanson and would want to talk to him soon. Since they did not have probable cause at this point, the two would put their heads together to figure out a way to convince him to come in for a visit.

The easy answer to all this was that the kidnappers found out where the money was from the Handelman sisters and paid Father Hastings a visit Monday night. However, the three men had a combined eighty-three years of experience in these matters, so they all knew that sometimes the easy answer was not always the correct one.

Chapter 29

Wednesday morning dawned cool and crisp but promised to be a beautiful late October day as the sun was shining accompanied by a light wind. Dick Mueller loaded up his gear into his truck and headed north out of Park Falls to enjoy the morning bowhunting for whitetail deer. He took a left turn onto an old logging road that skirted the eastern edge of the Chequamegon National Forest and parked in a turnaround about a quarter mile in. From there, the hike was about two hundred yards to a large oak tree where his portable tree stand would be set up about fifteen feet off the ground.

Dick climbed up, strapped himself in for safety, and towed up his gear up on a rope. After initial preparations, he settled in and enjoyed the commanding view of the landscape into which was carved several shooting lanes in case a deer would venture within thirty yards or so. This type of activity was therapeutic as he enjoyed the peaceful spectacle of the red squirrel and the woodpecker making winter preparations and marveled at the amount of noise these small animals could produce in the vast forest.

As the sun bathed his face, Dick reflected on how lucky of a man he was with his loving family and recent retirement. Soon a gentle breeze began blowing, making the environment very comfortable, which caused him to fall into an unplanned nap. A branch snapping in the distance woke him up. Being an experienced hunter, he moved nothing except his eyes. About one hundred yards out he spotted a large deer walking in his direction. He quietly drew back his bow and locked it into position. As the wind was blowing toward him, the deer did not pick up his scent and continued to move closer. It was obvious that this was no ordinary whitetail as he counted at least ten points on the antlers.

About twenty yards out, the deer turned broadside, presenting a dream scenario for any bow hunter, and Dick dialed in his aim on the heart. Just as the arrow was released, the animal flinched slightly and was struck a little above the target. The large buck took off in a full gallop eastward toward private land. Dick observed the path carefully, packed his equipment, and prepared for what could be a very long search.

As he reached the edge of the forest, some large patches of blood were found, which was encouraging as maybe the strike would prove fatal after all. While tracking through the dense woods, the blood trail became thicker but also crossed into private land. Entering was not a problem in this area as most landowners had a gentleman's agreement with hunters, allowing them to track a wounded animal through their property. The forest began to thin, and Dick could see a clearing with what looked like a hunting cabin on it. About twenty yards short of the cabin lay his trophy buck with its symmetrical ten-point rack and beautifully proportioned head, neck, and shoulders. He smiled broadly as this was positively the biggest whitetail to join his collection.

There was just one issue. The deer had decided to die on private land, and there was no way to tell if the cabin was occupied or not. The first task was to drag the buck back into the forest as he was sure the owner would not want it to bleed out in the clearing. After this, Dick approached the door and gave it five hard knocks before pausing. A female voice yelled for help, which chilled him to the bone.

"Who is in there, and are you all right?"

"It is Rita and Theresa Handelman. We are okay, but please call for help before they come back!"

"I will call right away!" Dick felt unnerved and could see that the hair was standing up on his arms as he went to the back of the cabin to check on the cell reception in the clearing. Thankfully, the cell responded, and he called 911.

"911, what is your emergency?"

"I have found Rita and Theresa Handelman. They are just off Meyers Road in a small hunting cabin. The door is locked, but the sisters have stated they are all right but need to get out! Please send some help."

"Oh my god, I will send help right away!"

"My name is Dick Mueller, and I was hunting in the area. I will hide in the woods to the right front of the cabin and will come out with my arms up. I am wearing hunting camouflage."

"Thank you so much, Mr. Mueller. I will let them know."

"Please come quickly."

Dick knocked on the door and told the ladies help was on the way and he would be staying until the police arrived. It was a long twenty minutes waiting in the woods wondering what he would do if someone other than the law pulled up. Thankfully, Sheriff Bosworth pulled in, followed closely by the ambulance and several other law enforcement vehicles. Dick came out of the woods with his hands up, and the sheriff waved him over.

"I did not break in, Sheriff, as the sisters said they were okay and thought it would be best if you did," began Dick. "It scared the shit out of me when those ladies cried for help when I knocked on the door. It's been an eventful day."

"Thanks, Mr. Mueller, you did the right thing," Sheriff Bosworth replied. "I can't tell you how much we appreciate your response and diligence. In case we have questions, I will take your cell phone number, but you are free to go."

"I have a strange request given the circumstances, Sheriff. I trailed a trophy buck into this clearing, which is how I discovered the Handelman sisters. Can I have permission to pick it up once I field dress the deer?"

"It's the least we could do. Once the deer is prepped, let me know, and I'll have one the deputies drive you back to your vehicle so you can come and pick it up."

Instead of trying to knock down the front door, a deputy broke the glass on the window in the back bedroom, crawled in, and unlocked it. Detective Allen, Agent Macklin, and the EMTs were the first to enter and found the ladies sitting in comfortable living room chairs but tied in so they couldn't get up. Theresa was silently rocking her head and shoulders back and forth. The cabin was heated, and there were dirty dishes and some food lying on the counter.

Rita broke down crying. "Oh, my god, thank you for coming. We need to get out of here before they come back!"

Detective Allen responded, "Rita, you and Theresa will be fine now. Who will come back, and what time do they come?"

"There are always two men. They come in the morning and then later in the afternoon. They take us one at a time and feed us and let us go to the bathroom, then strap us back in. We spend the nights alone!" Rita began crying again.

"It's all right, Rita, we will bring both of you to the hospital to get checked on, but you have nothing to fear as you will not be alone anymore. We will stop up later to talk to you if you are feeling up to it."

Agent Macklin had listened to this exchange and had a plan. All personnel went out to their vehicles and turned off the flashing lights. When Rita and Theresa were taken away by ambulance, the driver was instructed to not turn on the lights until he was closer to town. All people present, including Dick Mueller, were told to keep this quiet at least until this evening. Two Price County sheriff's deputies were left behind and told to wait in the cabin in case the perpetrators showed up for their afternoon visit.

Everyone congratulated Dick on his gorgeous trophy buck and thanked him for finding the Handelman sisters. With the exception of the two deputies, all others vacated the property as unobtrusively as possible. It was about 12:15 p.m., and Agent Macklin was betting that the kidnappers had not witnessed the rescue of the ladies.

Sheriff Bosworth called Paul and told him his aunts were safe but asked that they keep it quiet for the afternoon as there was a plan to apprehend the kidnappers. Paul thanked the sheriff, told Jill, and both broke down crying with relief. They would see Rita and Theresa tonight. The sheriff also called Connie Moore to have her schedule a press conference for 6:00 p.m. Good news had materialized this afternoon, and with any luck, there would be more to add.

Chapter 30

J ust before the Handelman sisters arrived at Park Falls Hospital, Father Hastings was discharged. He was now back to himself and was given a ride to the police station to pick up his vehicle and belongings. Father informed Chief Collins that he would only be spending Wednesday night at the hotel this week. After that, he would be riding down to Milwaukee for a Catholic priest's conference that lasted through Sunday. A return on Monday was planned at which time Father Hastings would check back into the station. Chief Collins made a note to himself to let Sheriff Bosworth know.

Rita and Theresa were first brought to the emergency room to check for any physical injury. Outside of a couple of bumps and bruises, they were in good shape. A private shared room was prepared, and the ladies were wheeled over where they were cleaned up, given some fresh garments, and fed a hot lunch, which they both devoured. Theresa was given some medicine for her condition and had stopped her back-and-forth rocking. Both ladies were significantly calmer when Agent Macklin and Detective Allen entered to ask a few questions. As Paul always said, they were nothing if not resilient.

Detective Allen began, "Hello, Rita and Theresa. First of all, we want to let you know you are safe here. We are so glad to see you and just wanted to ask you a few questions. Can you describe what happened on Sunday?"

Rita began, "Detective Allen, Theresa is dealing with Alzheimer's disease, so I will answer the questions. Our caregiver Lisa left around noon. We were going to take a nap and wait for Paul and Jill to pick us up for dinner at four. Sometime during this time, two men entered the house. Both had a mask on and demanded to know where the money was. We said we didn't have any money. They tied us to the kitchen chairs and went downstairs and started pounding on the walls. Finally, they untied us and said we were going with them. When they reached for me, Theresa grabbed a candleholder and hit one of them over the head. He took off his mask as he was bleeding, but I didn't recognize him. Theresa was contained, then they tied both of us up and walked us toward the vehicle and put us in the backseat. It looked like an older four-door Ford pickup truck, but I couldn't tell for sure."

Detective Allen stopped for a moment and called back to the sheriff's office so he could send a sketch artist.

"Did they hurt you at all while they were at your house?"

"Well, the men tied us up, and that hurt, but they did not strike us. Also, they did not talk much. Usually, just the smaller of the two men did the talking."

"When you got to the cabin what happened?"

"They had the place heated and let us sit in comfortable chairs but kept us tied up. As I stated earlier, twice a day, the men would be back to give us something to eat and let us go to the bathroom. We would be left alone from nightfall until the following day with just a small lamp in the corner and the heater going. We slept very little as we did not know what was coming next."

"Did you get to see their faces at all?"

"Yes, as it moved into the second day, it seemed they were less concerned with their identity, and both entered the home at different times without their masks. I glanced but then looked the other way, so they didn't suspect anything. When they realized it, the masks were quickly put back on."

"Did these men question you about the money?"

"A little bit, but we never told them where it was. We just kept saying we didn't know about any money. The men never threatened us, so we never told them much."

Agent Macklin summarized, "Rita, what I heard is that these men questioned you real hard about this money when they were at the house, but once you were back in the cabin, they didn't question you much? You never told them that Father Hastings had the money?"

Rita replied, "No, we never told them. We thought maybe they knew or were looking on their own and would get back and question us harder, but they never did."

The detective and agent glanced at each other as both were thinking this was not adding up. Typically, in these types of incidents, the victims were treated mercilessly until the information they were looking for was volunteered. This method would not have been that tough in the case of the Handelman sisters, yet it appeared the kidnappers never took that path. The sketch artist arrived, and Rita was able to give them height, weight, description, and facial profile of the two men.

"Thank you for your time and the information, Rita," closed Detective Allen. "Please rest up, and don't worry. We now have some information to go on and will continue to pursue these people." The men then made their way back to the sheriff's department.

Price County sheriff's deputies Scott Campbell and Seth Roberts remained at the cabin off Meyers Road. Deputy Campbell had set up inside on the left front of the cabin while Deputy Roberts covered the right. Their plan was to let the perpetrators come in a few steps then tell them to put their hands up and drop their weapons. One of them would then shut the door, and the men would be apprehended.

About 3:30 p.m., the deputies heard a vehicle coming up the drive. When they glanced out the window, it was an older Ford four-door pickup, but they could only see the driver.

"I only see one," said Deputy Campbell.

Deputy Roberts replied, "We need to take him anyway. The detectives can question him."

"How do we know it is someone associated with the kidnapping?"

Deputy Roberts did not answer until they saw the man slip on his mask. "That's how. Draw your weapon."

The door unlocked and the masked man entered, looked around for a second, realized the ladies were not in the cabin, and turned to leave.

Detective Roberts shouted, "Drop the weapon and put up your hands!"

The surprised intruder nearly jumped through the roof but obliged by raising his hands in the air.

"I have no weapon!"

The deputies pulled off his mask to reveal a tired-looking man in his thirties with an untreated fresh scar above one eye. Deputy Roberts frisked him, put cuffs on, and watched over the suspect while his partner called headquarters to report the news.

Allen, Macklin, and Bosworth all took a minute to digest the news and discuss what to do. Finally, Agent Macklin said, "Deputy Campbell, we are going to leave you there for about an hour to see if anyone else comes. According to the Handelman sisters, there were usually two. Do not interrogate him, but if he starts talking, keep the conversation going and take notes."

"Yes, sir."

Deputy Campbell read the Miranda rights to the apprehended suspect, who just stared straight ahead and did not say anything, causing the hour to pass very slowly. During this time, no other vehicles were arriving either. About 4:45 p.m., two police cars pulled up, and the man was transported to Sheriff's headquarters for questioning. Agent Macklin's plan had been successful in netting at least one of the suspects.

Chapter 31

Upon arriving at the Price County Sheriff's Headquarters, the suspect was transferred to an interrogation area near the jail. Detective Allen and FBI Agent Macklin would do the questioning while Sheriff Bosworth would observe.

"State your name, please."

"I won't be telling you anything until I get a lawyer, including my name."

The suspect did not have any identification with him, but Sheriff Bosworth got a good look and remembered seeing his face while reviewing files yesterday. This was Carl Hanson. Amy Sutherland's hunch was correct. He texted Agent Macklin the name.

"Well, Mr. Hanson, you don't need to answer that question anymore."

"How do you know my name?"

"We have ways. You have a relatively clean record but are not a stranger to run-ins with the law."

"I'm not saying anymore. I'm done until I get a lawyer."

"We will call the judge and make it happen. In the meantime, let me tell you a few facts of life. Tomorrow morning you will appear in court and be charged with two counts of felony kidnapping. Right now, you are looking at spending the rest of your life in prison. We also know that you were not solely responsible for this, you are just the first one caught. There was also a robbery committed at Father Hastings' residence a couple of nights prior that we suspect you may also be involved in. Add this all together, and you will not see the outside world again. Your cooperation would go a long way in helping out your cause. You think about that tonight as you wait in your cell, and we'll make sure there is a lawyer here tomorrow morning."

Carl Hanson remained silent as Detective Allen called the jailer to check him in and show him to his cell.

The time was approaching five thirty, and the three men discussed what they would release at the press conference. Sheriff Bosworth had also decided to entertain a few questions this time around. The local media affiliates were filing in, and Connie Moore convinced most of them to run a live feed on their evening newscast as there were some breakthroughs.

At promptly 6:00 p.m., Sheriff Bosworth began.

"Thank you for showing up on short notice tonight. We have some good news to share. Rita and Theresa Handelman have been found alive and well today. A local deer hunter who wishes to remain anonymous tracked a deer he shot to a clearing near a hunting cabin. When he knocked on the cabin door, he heard calls for help and alertly called 911. The ladies were rescued soon after and are now at Park Falls Hospital recuperating. There were no serious injuries, and a full recovery is expected.

"In addition, with the help of our department, FBI Agent Macklin executed a plan that nabbed one of the kidnappers. He is being held in the county jail and will be interrogated over the next few days. Please keep your eyes and ears open as there were two kidnappers, but we only have one in custody. This is a great day for law enforcement and our area. The collective prayers of everyone in Price County have been answered. Tonight I will stay and take a few questions."

The television outlets that were broadcasting cut the live feed at this point so their anchors could comment but continued to roll the tape for the late news. The questions then started and were all over the board as was typical with press conferences.

"Sheriff Bosworth, can you share the name of the suspect?"

"Not at this time."

"Has the break-in at Father Hastings residence been solved?"

"Not yet, we are still investigating."

"You said there were no serious injuries to the ladies, can you expand?"

"The Handelman sisters were held captive, so there were some injuries related to this. There were no physical injuries other than that. Rita and Theresa are hardy individuals, and it appears they will recover well."

"Isn't it a real stroke of luck that the hunter stumbled across the sisters?"

"I can't tell you how lucky it was. Amazing, and the gentleman who found them knew enough to do the right thing under pressure. I can't give him enough credit. As remote as the cabin is, it was almost like divine intervention."

"What are your plans now?"

"We will talk to the suspect and continue to investigate the new crime scene at the hunting cabin to see if we can find additional evidence. Also, we know there was at least one other person involved. The investigation will continue at Father Hastings' residence also."

"Do you think the two crimes are related?"

"As I said, they are still under investigation. A lot has happened in the last four days."

"Why do you think they were kidnapped?"

"I would think the rumors of the money that have been going around the area may have had a lot to do with it."

"What can you tell us about the money."

"Nothing as it is just the subject of rumors."

"You said at least one more involved. Are there more than two people involved?"

"Not that I know of at this time, but we are sure there are two."

Sheriff Bosworth received a glance from Agent Macklin that said it would be best to shut this down now.

"Anyone have anything else that we didn't cover yet? No? Thank you for coming. If we have any more developments, Connie will be in touch with you."

Sheriff Bosworth then called Judge William Hawkins at home to explain the developments and to check if he could have a public defender sent over on Thursday morning. Given the circumstances, the judge said to expect a lawyer bright and early as he would make a few calls. He would also schedule an arraignment hearing for the morning.

Chapter 32

"Are you alone and able to talk?"

"Yes."

"Did you watch the news at six o'clock?"

"Looks like we need to activate our contingency plan."

"Correct, we will expedite the time frame and arrive at our meeting spot earlier than scheduled. The contacts will be made aware."

"We need to get this moving now. When do we meet?"

"Six Friday night, which doesn't leave much time. I will be leaving tomorrow morning."

"Same here with some stops, but I will be there."

"Assuming you have your cargo?"

"Yes, and also assuming you have yours?"

"I have it also. Call this number if you run into delays or difficulties, but it is crucial we stay on track now due to the arrest today."

"I don't foresee any issues but will get in touch if something comes up."

"What are the odds, a fucking deer hunter stumbling across the sisters and then one of them getting caught. Unbelievable. I figured that was the most reliable part of our plan. Hopefully, he will hold out for a bit."

"I hear you, but that is why we had a backup plan. Nothing is ever easy. We wanted a diversion but not exactly this. However, it should still keep everyone occupied for a while."

"You are right. Even with this development, I still think we are good for a few days, and once we execute, there will be no worries."

"As long as we can trust all the contacts."

"We are making it worth their while and then some, so I have no doubt it will work out."

"Even if we wanted to, there is no pulling back now anyway."

"Right, sleep as well as you can, and we'll see you on Friday at six."

"You also, see you then."

Chapter 33

Father Hastings loaded up his Ford Explorer with everything in his hotel room and left for Milwaukee at 5:00 a.m. to attend the Catholic priests' conference at the downtown Sheraton. He checked into the hotel at 11:00 a.m. and signed into the conference in time to participate in the first seminar at noon, which was ironically entitled "Commitment to the Church." The session ended around 2:00 p.m., bringing most priests into the hall to socialize. Father Hastings went up to his hotel room to change clothes and promptly exited the conference to begin his drive south. He had twenty-eight hours to reach his destination.

The priest watched his speed and tucked in behind some over the road truck drivers for the journey. His age dictated more stops than desired for bathroom breaks, but these were timed with gas, food, and drink, so he continued to make good time. A busy truck stop in central Texas served as a resting point to take a two-hour nap, which was sorely needed. At 5:00 p.m., he pulled into Laredo, Texas. There was time to kill, so he picked up some fast food and coffee before arriving at the private home of the contact.

Walking to the residence after parking on the street, he noticed a black Mercedes Benz with Wisconsin license plates. His partner had arrived, indicating things were going as planned so far. They had a busy night of preparation in front of them before continuing the journey. Julio Juarez answered the door and let him in. Mr. Jaurez was in the business of moving people over the border. He found that over the years it was much more profitable moving Americans to Mexico than Mexicans to America. The Americans usually were flush with cash and running from the law, family, or something else, so they were willing to pay top dollar to get set up as a Mexican citizen and transported to their destination.

"The first thing we will do is have some of my men clean out your cars and bring your possessions into the house," began Julio. "This will include the money and any other loose objects. Next, we will drive these cars to a junkyard, remove the license plates, and have them crushed. We will need $5,000 for this."

"We weren't told about this," protested Lindsey Barrington.

Julio Juarez was a no-nonsense businessman.

"No, you weren't, and there are other expenses you will incur outside of the standard fee. You are on my turf now and will go along with us."

There were no further objections from either as they knew this was their only chance, but it was very uncomfortable being at the mercy of this man. After the goods were brought into the house and accounted for, a stack of one hundred dollar bills was handed to Julio along with the car keys. Two men drove away with the vehicles.

Next came a slight makeover for both. Lindsey's hair was short-ened and dyed blonde. Father Hastings had his parted hair trimmed into a crewcut and dyed darker to get rid of the gray. Pictures were taken for Mexican passports and citizenship documents. The tough-est part was the name change. Marie Lopez and George Hernandez were now de facto Mexican citizens. Two more stacks of hundreds were handed over for this service. Marie and George were instructed to give up any documents from the United States including driver's license, passports, and credit cards. These were thrown into a fire and burned.

Julio could detect the nervousness on the part of his guests.

"Marie and George, please relax. I am here to provide a service. I know how much money you have and have dealt with cases like this many times in the past. You and your money are safe as I want to continue my business. Marie, you heard about my reputation from someone you know. I do not want to ruin that. We will success-fully get each of you to your final destination with a nice, fat bank account. Try to get some rest as we will leave tomorrow morning around five for an early border crossing."

After Julio had left the room, the two looked at each other and laughed a little. George thought this was a good sign as they were still on the same wavelength. Plus, there was no going back now.

"Have you ever had blonde hair before? It looks like a pretty good cover."

"No, always a brunette, but it's fine. We have to take some precautions."

"How much money will these guys take from us? I wasn't crazy about the extra five thousand we had to cough up."

"Me either, but I would expect each stop will cost us, especially the bank as Julio told me that would be ten to twenty thousand. I'm sure it will be twenty. When we are finished, we will have dished out over one hundred thousand dollars, but that is the price you pay to do it right."

"Let's just hope our partners up north hold out for a little while."

"I'm sure they will be squealing as life in prison will not sound attractive. If it breaks loose next week, we should be well on our way. Have confidence. Julio will get it done for us."

Chapter 34

A t promptly 9:00 a.m. Thursday, Carl Hanson appeared before Judge Hawkins with his court-appointed lawyer, Jeff Henderson, where he was charged with two counts of felony kidnapping. Attorney Henderson pleaded not guilty at the request of his client. Judge Hawkins set the bail at one million dollars, which drew a half-hearted objection, but in the end, Mr. Hanson returned to his cell. He told his attorney he wouldn't be talking for a while.

The judge called Attorney Henderson into his chambers.

"Off the record, does your client truly understand the consequences here? A no-contest plea along with additional information provided could pave the way for a deal. He was caught red-handed and, if convicted, is looking at spending the rest of his life behind bars. Despite this, he is obstinate regarding cooperation."

"I can't say I know him, Judge. I'm just doing a favor for the county here in defending him. He does seem to have his heels dug in, and I'm not sure why. I'll continue to talk to him to see if we can loosen this up. Once a trial gets closer, I'm sure he will see the light."

"That may be a while. I encourage you to garner some cooperation in the meantime."

"I'll see what I can do."

The FBI and State of Wisconsin investigators had been busy also. They discovered that local businessman Mark Harwell owns the hunting cabin where the Handelman sisters were found. Mark was shocked when contacted and didn't know how anyone could have entered without breaking in. There was a key, but only family members knew where to find it. Investigators determined that Mark's son John works at GLK Industries in Park Falls. When the FBI called, they were informed that John Harwell had requested a few vacation days this week, which he planned to spend hunting and had returned to work on Thursday. Normally, this would raise no suspicion, but given the timing of his vacation combined with the events of the week, Detective Allen ordered a background check.

John Harwell did not have a clean record with law enforcement as the data showed a charge of embezzlement and theft when he had worked for another local business. His lawyer, Lindsey Barrington, somehow had this reduced to a misdemeanor, and John was placed on probation. The connection with Lindsey was just another puzzle piece that would be placed off to the side because, as of right now, the investigators were not sure where it fit in. However, they definitely wanted to talk to John and began looking at the sketches Rita Handelman had provided. The description along with the sketch matched up somewhat to the photo they had on record, but this was not enough to go on. The day would be spent building a case in an attempt to make an arrest on Friday.

Paul and Jill Handelman visited their aunts on Thursday again and were given news from the doctor that they could go home as soon as Friday. A home security system would be installed that day, and the sisters seemed in good spirits. Theresa's dementia was still there, but she was talking a little bit now.

Paul asked, "Are you comfortable going back home after what happened?"

"Yes, we want to get back to our routine, Pauly," responded Rita. "I know we will have to start looking for other arrangements or more help, but we want to get back home."

"If you are ready, we will help you out. The sheriff's department said they would keep someone on watch for a week or two."

"Yes, we are ready, Pauly. We have seen a lot in our lives and just want to go back home now for a while."

"Great, we'll make that arrangement for tomorrow morning. Jill and I will pick you up and give you a ride back home. We will also call Jen and Lisa and have them resume their care starting Friday evening."

Detective Allen and Agent Macklin knocked at the door.

"Rita and Theresa, could we have you look at some pictures to see if any of these men look familiar?"

The ladies looked through four profile pictures, and both picked out the photo of John Harwell.

"He was one of them at the house when we were taken," replied Theresa. "He kept an eye on us while the other one drove and talked."

Paul thought it was great to hear Theresa this lucid.

"That is correct," said Rita. "He was one of them. We saw him without his mask a few times."

"Thanks, ladies, can you please sign this statement regarding the photo? We will continue to gather more evidence," stated Detective Allen, who immediately called the crime lab.

"This is Allen. We have an urgent request that involves the fingerprints collected from Rita and Theresa Handelman's home. John Harwell is in the database, and we need to know tonight if any of these prints belong to Mr. Harwell." Sheriff Bosworth assured the men that the prints combined with identification by the Handelman sisters would be enough to arrest the suspect in the morning. After an hour, the crime lab called to verify a match with one set of prints pulled from the kitchen at Handelman Hill.

Chapter 35

John Harwell had just finished packing his lunch for work early Friday morning when he heard a knock at his front door. Assuming it was one of the neighbors, he answered to find himself face-to-face with two sheriff's deputies along with several investigators. Deputy Campbell served the search warrant while his partner performed the arrest, which was met with no resistance. Detective Allen and his team began their work. Predictably, John Harwell also requested a lawyer to represent him and called a family friend, Gerald Cooper.

The findings included $20,000 in cash along with the address of a cabin on nearby Butternut Lake. According to records, this property was owned by Lindsey Barrington's brother, but John Harwell would need to shed some light on this discovery. However, Attorney Cooper stated that he was not talking at this time.

On Friday afternoon, Judge Hawkins followed suit from the morning and charged the second suspect with two counts of felony kidnapping to start with accompanied by one million dollars in bail. Breaking and entering along with armed robbery would probably follow soon based on the discovery of the cash. The plea was not guilty, and again, Judge Hawkins called Attorney Cooper into his chambers where he was joined by Attorney Henderson.

"Gentlemen, off the record again, of course, the evidence is mounting, and your boys are in trouble here. There are a number of things being discovered that tie the two crimes together. We need some cooperation from these fellows. I would encourage you to have them assist the investigators, and we can lower the charges."

"What are you thinking, Judge?"

"It depends. If the crime involved others and they tell the story, we can give them five to ten probably for cooperating as long as they are telling the truth. That beats life multiplied by two or three. If they did this alone and can save us the trouble of the trials, maybe ten to twenty. This town has been through enough, and we need some answers."

"Well, we can let them sit for the day and think about it. We'll tell Carl that his partner is also in custody."

"All right, when they are ready, you let me know, and I'll contact law enforcement to get a confession."

Cooper and Henderson both met with their clients to tell them the game was up and both could help their cause by talking. The more information provided, the better chance they would have at leniency. Carl Hanson acted surprised when told that his partner was now in custody. While the men knew each other, neither knew how the other would react. The last thing they wanted was to have this pinned on them individually while the other received a break. Both men asked their lawyers to contact them each day, and it seemed like they might be opening up to the idea of telling their story.

Attorney Cooper called his good friend Mark Harwell.

"Mark, this is Gerry, do you have some time to talk?"

"I guess so, what in the hell is going on here? Is John tied up with all this shit that we are hearing about?"

"It appears that way. Neither one of them is talking, and they are facing life. What has been going on with John lately that would have made him get involved with this?"

"Well, he is having some issues with his marriage and is currently separated, so that isn't helping. Also, I'm not sure, but maybe he is tied up with meth again. I don't know."

"He is up to eyeballs in trouble right now and needs to cooperate soon. There was some relatively heavy action going on the last week, and knowing these two, quite frankly, I don't think they have the mental capacity to coordinate all this. But you never know as they did get caught."

"Are you saying you think others may be involved or may have hired them?"

"That's my suspicion, but they will need to come clean soon. Hard time is a certainty even with a confession, but the difference may be a few years instead of the rest of their lives. As each day passes, Judge Hawkins will grow more impatient, which will add to the difficulty of seeking leniency. He is in no mood."

"Our relationship isn't the greatest, but I will go over there Saturday to see if I can talk with him."

"I'll go with you. Maybe the two of us can convince him to talk. Sorry, Mark, but we'll do the best we can."

"Sounds good. Thanks, Gerry. I need to let the rest of the family know what is happening as I'm sure this will be on the news tonight."

Chapter 36

M arie Lopez and George Hernandez were woken up at 4:00 a.m. Saturday to prepare for their busy day. The first step would be to cross the border into Nuevo Laredo, Mexico. Traffic was light at this early hour as Julio picked out the second checkpoint station on the right. The Mexican border guard accepted an envelope from him and radioed ahead, so the three Mexican citizens were allowed to continue on their way without being waved over for a search. The critical first step was complete, with the drive continuing to Monterrey for a 9:00 a.m. appointment with Rafael Castillo to set up bank accounts at Banco Azteca.

Upon arrival, Julio was instructed to drive to the back of the building through a garage door usually used by armored carriers to exchange cash. The two duffel bags of American currency were moved to a back room where Rafael met with all three. "I understand you have some US dollars that you would like to use to establish new bank accounts as Mexican citizens?"

"That is correct," stated Julio. "This is Marie Lopez and George Hernandez who would each like a separate account as they will not be residing together."

Rafael looked at the papers, which were in order, and proceeded to set up an account for each. "How much cash would you like to keep, and would you like pesos or dollars?"

Marie and George looked at each other as they hadn't thought about this.

"$50,000 each with $10,000 converted to pesos and $40,000 left in US dollars," replied Julio, who looked at his customers. "It is beneficial to have some cash as the banks sometimes are not as dependable as they are back in the United States. Also, we will have more fees to pay."

"You will also need to pay $10,000 each to set up these accounts, so we'll keep $120,000 out," replied Rafael. "I assume you want to split the rest?"

"Yes, divide the rest evenly," replied Julio, who had been instructed to do this. He detected that Marie and George were again getting extremely nervous.

"Relax, my friends! You will soon have legitimate bank accounts, and the funds will be available. Rafael will set up an ATM card for each of you, and we will try it out later today. Your money is in our banking system but is available to you, just as it would be in the United States. A statement will be generated indicating the value of each account once we are finished."

Marie and George opened up accounts worth 1.88 million dollars each. For the former residents of northern Wisconsin, this amount of money was breathtaking. Once the statement was shown, and the ATM cards were received, the two calmed down a bit. They were each given a name of a Banco Azteca contact in the area that they would be residing and welcomed to Mexico. Everyone was happy as more American cash moving into Mexico was always a good thing down here. Their next destination was a home in Guadalajara where they would spend the night before splitting up the next day to complete their journey. Roberto Mendoza, one of Julio's business partners, was the owner of the residence.

"Roberto, how are you, my friend," stated Julio as the front door opened.

"Doing well, Julio. Go ahead and park in the back. Come in and introduce me to our newest Mexican citizens!"

The long day of riding along with the realities of their new life had Marie and George looking a bit frazzled. After introductions, Roberto said, "No worries, my friends! As Julio told you, we are in the business of safely setting you up as new citizens. It has been a long day, so please join us for wine or tequila before we eat dinner. We will then discuss tomorrow's plans."

After an excellent dinner and a couple of drinks, everyone was in a peaceful state as Roberto revealed final plans.

"Marie, you will leave with a driver tomorrow morning around 8:00 a.m. and complete your journey to Puerto Vallarta where you will be checked in at the Hilton Resort. A hotel room has been reserved for you for one month. Here is the card of a real estate agent that can help you find a permanent residence.

"George, you will leave around the same time for Zihuatanejo and will be checked into the Aura del Mar Hotel where we have also reserved a room for one month. Here is the card of a real estate agent in the area to help with finding your permanent residence.

"You will not have to pay our drivers as it is included in the $10,000 fee you will each pay me tonight, but it wouldn't hurt to throw them a $100 tip. The price includes your transportation to the final destination and a month's stay in the hotels. After that, you are on your own. You are in no danger of being discovered unless you have revealed your plans to others back home. I can't help you with that. Julio and I, along with our employees, take a vow of silence, so after we drop you off, you no longer exist in our minds. You are safe."

George and Marie handed over $10,000 each to Roberto and thanked him and Julio for everything. The 1.88 million in their bank accounts made the cash exchange less of an issue. They had spent a lot of money, but it appeared they were going to achieve the end goal.

Julio closed out the evening.

"Marie and George, welcome to Mexico." All four raised their glasses to celebrate with some twenty-one-year-old barrel-aged Patron tequila. "As my friend Roberto and I have been telling you, we would like to stay in business and will forget all about you once tomorrow comes. You are now Mexican citizens and are free to travel although I would strongly advise staying away from the United States for obvious reasons. You will do yourself a favor by learning some basic Spanish also.

"We expect you to also forget about us, our names, the fact we ever met, everything. Our three-day business transaction will close tomorrow. Please treat it as such, and if you run into trouble, remember, we never existed. If we find out that you have exposed any of the people you have met during this journey, we will eliminate you. No questions asked. Plain and simple. We do have methods of finding this out, so on the way to your new homes, purge everything from your mind, and there will be nothing to worry about."

Chapter 37

J udge William Hawkins was getting ready to attend Sunday Mass
when he received a call from Attorney Cooper informing him that
both clients were willing to tell their story. They would also like to
change their plea to "no contest" and accept whatever penalty the
courts saw fit. Both lawyers spent Saturday trying to convince their
clients to confess as the evidence against each was getting to be overwhelming. Late in the evening, the two changed their minds, so it
was decided to wait until Sunday morning to hear their version of
the events.

Detective Allen and FBI Agent Macklin were called in to direct
the interview and were excited to learn of the confession. They had
spent the previous day going over all the evidence, which included a
number of puzzling soft references to Lindsey Barrington but nothing that solidly brought it all together.

Carl Hanson and John Harwell along with their attorneys
joined the law enforcement agents in the conference room along with
a court reporter who was also called in to record the proceedings.

Detective Allen started, "I understand that each of you would
like to tell your story. Mr. Hanson, could you please describe the
events from the day of the kidnapping until you were apprehended?"

Carl began, "John and I pulled up to the house around two
Sunday afternoon. We expected we would need to break in, but the
garage door was open. We went right into the house and surprised
the sisters, who were sleeping. We knew time was limited, so we tied
them up on the kitchen chairs and checked downstairs for money.
We banged on a few walls, opened some doors, but did not find any

money. We then took them with us. I was hit above the eye by one of them with something that caused a cut. We took them to the cabin where you found them on Wednesday. Each day we would show up twice to feed them and allow them to use the bathroom."

John Harwell was fidgeting a little.

Detective Allen asked, "John, was that an accurate portrayal or did you have something to add."

"It was accurate, but as long as we are confessing, let's confess. We were hired by Lindsey Barrington for this job. She promised us some money along with erasing any legal issues we currently have with the law if we followed through.

"The money you found in my house was the payment from Lindsey. Also, we were the ones that were involved in the robbery at Father Hastings' house. This wasn't a robbery but a staged event where we slightly injured Father Hastings and took the money. We ransacked the house to make it look like a crime. The money was taken to a cottage on Butternut Lake as directed."

"Was Father Hastings a part of this or just a victim?"

"He was a part of it. Lindsey directed all the action, but Father definitely knew what was coming and what we were doing."

"He's at a conference in Milwaukee and should be back in town tomorrow."

"I doubt if he will be back. I have no idea where they were going, but they were going somewhere with the money."

"How long were you planning to keep Rita and Theresa in the cabin?"

"We were instructed to call police a week later, which would be today and disclose their whereabouts."

FBI Agent Macklin summed up, "John and Carl, I am hearing you say you were hired to kidnap Rita and Theresa Handelman and keep them hidden for a week and then let them go. In the meantime, you were moving money for Lindsey Barrington and Father Hastings who were going somewhere with this cash. Does that seem to cover it?"

"Yes," both said simultaneously.

"Why did you sign up for something like this?"

Carl Hanson began, "I heard rumors of this money like everyone else. It's always tough to make ends meet with the job that I have, and extra cash would go a long way. The plan sounded easy enough when explained, and we would not be hurting or killing anyone."

John Harwell added, "Same here. The money would come in handy. Lindsey is also very persuasive and made it sound like what we were doing was nothing, and we would be rewarded well for it. She also stated that it was almost impossible to get caught, so we would just be moving on with life after we called the police. The money we received blinded me to how terrible the kidnapping was. We did not realize this until a couple of days in. Even though we were arrested, part of me was glad the sisters were discovered early on as I don't know if I could have continued that treatment for a week."

Detective Allen asked, "Why did you wait until now to confess? You were both very uncooperative in the early stages and have now told us everything."

There was an uncomfortable silence, and both bowed their heads. Then Carl said, "We were told that if caught early we should hold out until Sunday if possible."

FBI Agent Macklin kicked in. "Your delay may result in the suspects getting away. One of the conditions of your plea bargain is that the suspects were to be identified and located. You have identified, but if we don't locate either, I'm not sure what will happen regarding sentencing."

At this point, Attorney Cooper spoke, "The men told you everything they know. That was the agreement. They committed the crime but were hired to do so. I'm not sure if locating either one is possible at this point, but they have held up their end of the bargain."

"The frustration is coming out as I suspect that Lindsey Barrington and Father Hastings are long gone, so I apologize for that. Carl and John, do you have anything else you wish to add?"

Carl was silent, but John stated, "No, nothing except I am sorry I was involved, and I hope the ladies are all right."

During this time, Sheriff Bosworth had called down to Milwaukee, and the police department would go over to the Sheraton to check on Father Hastings. Lindsey Barrington had a sign on her door stating she would be out of town but would be back in the office Monday. As the officials talked it over, there was stunned resignation that they might be too late.

Agent Macklin stated, "Hiding in plain sight. We all had hunches about Father Hastings and the extent of his injuries. Then these miscellaneous events regarding Lindsey Barrington."

Sheriff Bosworth replied, "Sounds like this was all set up as a diversion. Well, with the volume of episodes it certainly worked if they were looking to buy time for a week. We did have some feelings that things were not right, but in all fairness, it would have been tough to string it all together amid all the chaos."

Detective Allen closed, "The fact that Father Hastings had this money to start with related to the incidents that took place is still puzzling. If he had it, why didn't he leave on his own?"

Chapter 38

Ten days earlier...

F ather Hastings answered the doorbell at his home about 9:00 p.m. to find Lindsey Barrington standing on his doorstep.

"Ms. Barrington, what can I do for you?"

"Cut the bullshit, Father, and let me in. We need to talk about this money."

Father Hastings closed the door behind her, and both walked back to the kitchen to talk.

"Lindsey, I just received this money yesterday, and I plan to use it for good purposes throughout the area."

"I don't trust you. I think you are taking off with this money. Let me make it clear, I'll be watching your every move, and if you leave town with this, I'll be on your tail."

Father Hastings became a little obstinate. "This is my money now, why should I care what you think?"

"What I think is that Father Hastings would like to leave with this money, but he doesn't know where to go or how to get there without getting caught. Am I getting warm?"

"I know where I want to go. I would like to go somewhere like Zihuatanejo and start a new life away from the church. This would give me the opportunity."

"How would you do this? Just go driving over the border with $4 million in cash? You wouldn't make it fifty miles without getting murdered."

"I admit, it is a problem that I am trying to get an answer to."

"Father, $4 million is a lot of money. More than enough for three or four people. Plus, you can't keep this in your home for much longer, and who knows what the government would do if they found out about it."

"What are you saying?"

"I have an answer, but I need to be in for half."

"That's two million, for what? What are you going to provide?"

"Safe passage and a new life in Mexico. Seems a small price to pay. I will go along with you to a point, but I have my own Mexican dreams."

"How would this work?"

"I have made some contacts, and for about $80,000 to $100,000 each, we can both get a new identity, become Mexican citizens and open up two legitimate bank accounts. All we have to do is find a way to get everything down to Laredo, Texas."

"And may I ask how you know people who do this? What inspired you to pursue to this level?"

"As I stated, I have my dreams and know of people who have made this type of move in the past. They hooked me up with their contacts."

"Do we just pick a day and drive down? What if people contacted us during this time?"

"Precisely, we need a five-day period for this to develop, so it would be best if we left when no one was suspecting it and other activities were occupying the community. We need to create a diversion, which will take the attention off us."

"I hate to ask, but what do you have in mind?"

"A kidnapping of the Handelman sisters followed closely by a staged robbery of your home. Once executed, we pick a time and go."

"You would go through all this just for a diversion? Do you realize we would be interviewed once the kidnapping takes place and after the robbery? This sounds crazy!"

"Once again, yes. It is perfect really. Once the interviews are complete and there is nothing on us, we will be out of the spotlight for a while. That is when we leave for Texas."

"Are you sure we couldn't do this without the so-called diversion? It seems excessive. Who would kidnap the ladies and take care of them? How long would they be held captive?"

"I know a couple of guys who could use the money and would do this for us for about $20,000 each. One of them has a remote family cabin where the ladies could be held. The police would be informed the following Sunday."

Silence ensued for a few minutes as Father Hastings soaked this all in.

"I'll be honest with you, Lindsey. This money is really tearing me up. I can hardly sleep at night, and I don't know whether to take all or part of it, but I know I want some on my own."

"Now is the perfect time to strike because hardly anyone knows the money is here. I just found out today when I called Rita to ask her about it. I have it set up for 2:00 p.m. on Sunday right during the Packer-Bear game. They should be able to get in and out without anyone knowing."

"You have it set up already? What if I say no?"

"I will cancel, but let's look at the timing. Right after the interviews regarding the kidnapping are finished, we will stage the robbery at your house. I expect this to be Monday or Tuesday evening."

"I have a conference in Milwaukee on Thursday, so Monday would work best."

"Now you are coming around. We'll see on the timing. You will be robbed and will have someone hit you lightly on the head to make it look like they knocked you out. That is what you will tell everyone including the doctors. Once you are released, hopefully, next day, you can tell them you will be driving to Milwaukee for a conference. Half the money will go with you. We will plan to meet in Laredo on Saturday evening, but if something goes haywire with our plan, we will meet on Friday. We should be in our new destinations by Sunday or Monday."

"The conference would be a good cover if I can check in and attend at least one seminar."

"Ideal, and I am just letting everyone know I am off Thursday and Friday and will be back in the office Monday."

"I can't imagine the kidnappers getting away with it forever, what happens if they get caught?"

"I will tell them to hold out until Sunday if caught early. Then they can tell the story. We will be long gone. Do not tell anyone where you are going, and we will be fine. If they play their cards right and have some luck, they may get away with this."

"I still believe it would be better just for the two of us to leave. Then no crime is committed. We just are missing, and the search would begin for us."

"That's exactly why we need to have a diversion. After a while, the authorities will suspect we are involved. However, it will take some time for them to start searching for us with all the chaos. If we go on our own, they will know it's us by Monday or Tuesday, but then a much wider net is cast as they wouldn't know if we went willingly or were kidnapped ourselves."

"You have really put some time and effort into this. I can't believe I am saying this, but let's go ahead. I do not know how to start this or how to break away, so let's follow your plan. A diversion would be good as the town would be less focused on this money. I worry that people will break in every night."

"You are lucky no one knows you have it, or I think you may be right. I'll work on the details and keep you posted."

Lindsey left with a smile as she had no idea how the priest would react to this plan and really did not know if he was going to flee or not. The cold October wind that stung her face was no bother as she would be living in paradise in less than two weeks.

Chapter 39

Cool air and bright sunshine graced Guadalajara on Sunday morning. Marie and George thanked their hosts and said their goodbyes. There would be no exchange of contact information at this time as each was destined for their version of paradise. George loaded his gear into a newer model Chevy Suburban and climbed into the front seat next to his driver Carlos. It would be a full day of somewhat leisurely travel with a few stops to see the sights along the way to Zihuatanejo.

As with all of Julio's employees, Carlos spoke perfect English.

"Do you mind if I turn on some music, George? It makes the drive happier."

"Not at all, Carlos, listen to what you would like."

Mexican polka music began to fill the vehicle as Carlos exhibited his excellent bilingual skills by singing along in Spanish. George figured if Carlos were happy, the drive would go smoother.

"George, what do you know about Zihuatanejo?"

"Not much, Carlos, other than it is a beautiful village along the bay with some fine fishing. It is also right next to Ixtapa, a popular resort area."

"You are right about that. The fishing is great. But what makes Zihuatanejo special is the people. They welcome everyone. There is a pretty good population of ex-Americans and ex-Europeans living there, and they blend in well with the locals. Also, the view from the hills overlooking the harbor is fantastic. The nice thing is, you can purchase housing and maid service for a very fair price, which is not the case in a lot of other coastal areas. Your money will go a long way. And no one bothers you in Z, they all mind their own business."

"That's good to know, Carlos, thanks for the info. I did a lot of fishing back home and can't wait to try some deep-sea fishing down here. Sounds like my kind of place."

The volume of the Mexican polkas increased, and Carlos continued to accompany the music with his singing. George reclined his seat back and reflected on the events of the last few days. It was mind-numbing what had transpired as Father Hastings ceased to exist and George Hernandez was now a permanent Mexican citizen. Thoughts of this type of transformation had been in his mind for a long time, but actually achieving it was another thing. He was feeling kind of proud of himself for his playacting during the interview and after the robbery. It was like a big game. Surprisingly, almost no thought was given to what the church, parish members, friends, or family would think. Until now, even George did not know how deep his desire for a different life was. The feeling of a new beginning in Mexico was like breaking out of chains.

A smile came to his face when thinking of the diversion involving kidnapping and robbery. Using 20-20 hindsight, he was sure this was completely unnecessary as they were missing either way. In fact, if they happened to get caught now, there would be a criminal conviction for kidnapping. George shook his head and thought about how uncomfortable the money made him and also the poor decisions he made as it was always on his mind. Any logic would tell you to try to sneak out of the country without committing a crime, yet he and Lindsey were convinced at the time they needed a criminal diversion to pull it off. A classic example of how greed can poison your thought process, and the Lord knows they both wanted that money. All is well that ends well though.

As they entered Zihuatanejo from the eastern hills, the view of the harbor was stunning as the sun was beginning to set. At last, they pulled into the Aura del Mar Hotel located right on the beach.

"Beautiful place, George," stated Carlos as he helped unload his luggage. "Enjoy the stay and don't worry about anything. Mexico will be a wonderful home for you."

George handed Carlos $200. "Thanks for everything, Carlos. I am looking forward to it."

Marie started her shorter journey to Puerto Vallarta by joining her driver Juan in a white Cadillac Escalade, occupying the passenger seat. Juan asked Lindsey for any music preferences as satellite radio was available. She chose Classic Vinyl on Sirius XM and cruised down the road with Juan listening to Led Zeppelin, Yes, Bruce Springsteen, and the like.

Juan asked, "Marie, are you familiar with Puerto Vallarta?"

"Only through vacations. I fell in love with the view of the bay as well as the moderate temperatures and trade winds that turn on like a clock in the early afternoon. It was so free and easy. We go on vacations to forget our real lives temporarily, and I was able to do that with ease in Puerto Vallarta."

"Yes, it is a great mix of traditional Mexican culture combined with a comfortable atmosphere for tourists. The housing market is growing rapidly, so you may have to pay a pretty good price for a place overlooking the bay, but prices will continue to rise, so that will be a sound investment for you. The views from the hillside homes are simply spectacular. Also, there are a lot of former Americans living there. Golf, tennis, fishing, and all sorts of other activities are readily available. Not to mention the sun shines over three hundred days each year."

"I think it shines about one hundred days a year in Wisconsin if we are lucky, Juan, so I am more than ready to start my new life."

It had been a long couple of weeks, so Marie put her seat back a couple of clicks, closed her eyes, and thought about the events that had taken place. She wondered how everyone would react when they discovered that she and Father Hastings had pulled this off. Oh, how the rumors would fly about them being involved with each other and running off together. She laughed at the thought of this. Marie was proud of herself for orchestrating the diversion and actually convincing Father Hastings to go along with it. Little thought was given to Carl Hanson and John Harwell, who were just a couple of pawns used to make her machine run. Since the Handelman sisters were safe, Marie figured the authorities wouldn't waste a great deal of time searching for her. No harm, no foul. She was still a little pissed that all the money was not in her possession, but at least there was 1.88 million.

Back home, what was left behind went to her brother, which represented partial payment for the use of his cabin during this adventure. Her thoughts turned to Sheila as they had not spoken for a while. If her partner had shown more commitment to taking the money, they could have teamed up together, but she knew Sheila would never do anything like that. Marie wondered what made the priest tick. To leave a lifetime of service and run the other way was really out of the ordinary. The one negative was the fact that returning to the United States was out of the question. But Marie would give it a go in Puerto Vallarta and not worry about these details for now. The sunshine and tennis courts were waiting.

The Escalade climbed some rather steep hills, and as they came over the rise, there lay Puerto Vallarta in all its sun-soaked glory. Juan unloaded the luggage at the Hilton, which had a commanding view of the bay.

"Marie, enjoy your stay and don't worry about a thing. Mexico will be a wonderful home for you."

Marie handed Juan $100 and stated, "Thanks, Juan, I will enjoy. I am ready to start fresh."

Chapter 40

The Milwaukee County sheriff's office called Sheriff Bosworth around 6:00 p.m. Sunday. They had interviewed hotel personnel as well as the Catholic priests that organized the conference. Father Hastings had attended a seminar on Thursday afternoon, but that was it, which did not strike the conference organizers as out of the ordinary because attendance was optional and several priests only showed up for one or two sessions. Hotel personnel stated a Do Not Disturb sign was found each day on Father Hastings' door, so they honored the request. When the room was entered Sunday afternoon, it had the appearance of never being used. Sheriff Bosworth feared that John Harwell was correct and they won't be seeing Father Hastings anytime soon.

Equally fruitless was the search for Lindsey Barrington. When they knocked on the door of her house, there was no answer. At this point, the police did not have a search warrant so could not enter. The sheriff's department did contact Josie Waters, her paralegal, who informed them that Lindsey was out of town. Josie would be opening up the office Monday morning and expected Lindsey back in the afternoon as they needed to prepare for a court case on Wednesday. As frustrating as it was, the investigators had no choice except to wait until Monday. At that time, they could obtain search warrants for Lindsey's home and office. Law enforcement would also know whether either would return as both were expected back in town.

Evidence from the investigations of the cabin off Meyers road and the cottage on Butternut Lake was also starting to come in. From the looks of it, everything so far backed up the stories told by Carl

Hanson and John Harwell. It had been one hell of a week. Sheriff Bosworth, Detective Allen, and Agent Macklin gathered in the conference room to determine where to go from here.

"I know one thing," started Agent Macklin, "I won't be eating pizza anytime soon after this investigation. Don't get me wrong, it is excellent, but I can't wait to get back to a routine."

Sheriff Bosworth responded, "I hear you there. How long will the FBI be involved in this? We have two perpetrators in custody, and the victims are back home unharmed. What type of effort will be put forth to find Barrington and Hastings?"

"I'm not sure, John. I'm scheduled to call the field office tomorrow and get their recommendation. I don't think I will be around here for much longer, but I need to determine how much assistance we can provide. What are your thoughts on the situation?"

"Well, our worlds turned upside down for a week, and a part of me would like to chase them to the ends of the earth. I'm sure others would agree. The pragmatist in me says they are long gone, probably south of the border somewhere. How much effort should be expended into chasing down two people who orchestrated a kidnapping in which the victims are unharmed?"

"I don't even know if we can charge them with anything regarding the money as it was in Father Hastings' possession," stated Detective Allen. "The kidnapping charge is serious, but there are certainly bigger challenges in the state and country that will require everyone's attention."

Sheriff Bosworth responded, "Agreed. Their biggest crime will be if they do not show up tomorrow as scheduled. A church, law office, and a lot of friends and family will be in disarray. I just don't know."

"We don't have to decide right now, gentlemen, as we are all tired," stated Agent Macklin. "Tired physically, mentally, and tired of this case. But state and local authorities should finish up the gathering of evidence. We probably have two more stops coming for Lindsey Barrington, so that will take a bit. Then this should be cataloged and summarized by the state. If Hastings or Barrington do not return, the FBI can issue a bulletin indicating they were involved in a kidnapping and are wanted. If we think they fled south of the border, we could have our friends in Mexico check a few things, but given the fact the victims are unharmed, it will probably not rise to the level of urgency needed. In reality, if they are down there, they are safe, unless they would be foolish enough to come back. The time required to investigate ex-patriates that leave for Mexico is astronomical, so I seriously doubt the FBI would be involved too deeply in this case."

Detective Allen added, "Unfortunately, I agree with Tom. There is so much horrible shit going on in the world we won't have the manpower to pursue this much further. We will put together the rest of the case, along with reports, and leave it at that. Unless your field office tells you to chase them down, Tom, I think this may be the end of the road, at least for now."

Sheriff Bosworth sighed. "At least we apprehended two of them involved even though they were hired hands. If Hastings and Barrington don't show up tomorrow, I'll begin preparing a final press conference, which we can hold Monday night. I will tell you though. This one will always be in the back of my mind."

"They were either extremely smart, lucky, or a little of both," stated the detective. "I was baffled as to why they put together a diversion at all, but our conversation today answered that. If they were just missing, the search would be much more intense starting tomorrow. Also, not harming the victims seemed to be by design, which also worked in their favor."

Agent Macklin added, "It was definitely out of the ordinary pattern of kidnappings, that is for sure. The good thing is, no one was hurt or killed. The kidnappers will need to serve some time due to stupidity, but that seems to be the biggest legal casualty. Anyone want that last piece of pizza?"

The three shared a long overdue good laugh before returning to their offices.

Chapter 41

Josie Waters opened up Lindsey Barrington's law office at 9:00 a.m. on Monday to begin case preparation for a Wednesday trial. Around nine thirty, the bell rang as the front door opened to reveal several investigators and a sheriff's deputy holding a search warrant.

"Ms. Waters, we have a court order to conduct a search of Lindsey Barrington's office in connection with the kidnapping of Rita and Theresa Handelman."

"What are you talking about? Lindsey was not involved in the kidnapping and was out of town the last few days," stated Josie.

"We can't get into details, Ms. Waters, but there is evidence your boss was involved. You can stay if you like but are also free to go."

"I will stay as I need to work on a case, and Lindsey will be back this afternoon. I'll be in the back room."

The detectives began looking through the file cabinets for any relevant evidence. Because of the volume of records, they would be busy for a while. By the time mid-afternoon came around, Josie was starting to worry as Lindsey had not shown up yet, so she broke the rule given to her and called Lindsey's cell phone. A message stated the number was not in service right now. Josie called over the deputy.

"I'm scared as Lindsey did not pick up her phone. Do you know what happened to her?"

"I cannot tell you, Ms. Waters, other than she is a suspect, and we are not surprised she failed to show up today. If you have a trial Wednesday, you may want to call the judge to get an extension."

Josie was now crying. "What is going on here? Is it all right if I go home? I know nothing about this!"

"Yes, Ms. Waters, you can go home if you wish, but please leave your phone number and the keys to the office. We will have more information for you by tomorrow."

Since it was mid-afternoon, a couple of the investigators started working at Lindsey Barrington's home. They entered by breaking through the garage service door to find the house almost entirely cleaned out except for the furniture and some bags of clothes. All personal items had been removed, so they wouldn't be spending too much time here. It was quite clear that Lindsey would not be returning.

Lindsey's brother, Tom Barrington, lived in Minneapolis and was contacted by phone as his cabin at Butternut Lake had been used during the crime. The detectives had found a few prints but little else and suspected these belonged to the perpetrators, Lindsey or Father Hastings.

"Mr. Barrington, this is Detective Allen of the Wisconsin Department of Criminal Investigation. Do you have a few minutes to chat?

"I do. What is the reason for your call? Did something happen to my sister?"

"Well, she is a suspect in the kidnapping of Rita and Theresa Handelman, and there is evidence that your cabin on Butternut Lake was used by the perpetrators."

"What happened? I don't know anything about this."

"We wouldn't expect you to. We have learned that Lindsey and another suspect hired a couple of locals to kidnap the Handelman sisters, and there is a good chance she has left the country, probably for good."

"Let me absorb this for a minute, Detective Allen." After a slight pause, Tom continued, "If you don't know this, I'm sure you will find it out soon, so I'll tell you now. Lindsey transferred most of her assets to me recently stating that she was going to be changing up her life a bit. I let her use my cabin anytime, but the amount transferred to me was much more than that was worth. I thought maybe she was not feeling well, but as is typical with Lindsey, she did not get into detail and just told me what was going to happen. I've learned over the years that it is an exercise in futility to argue with her."

"As we stated, Tom, this is what we think happened. Has she ever mentioned leaving the country for good? Where did she like to vacation?"

"She always liked Mexico for vacations, but I never heard her talk about leaving for good."

"Well, as of now she is a missing person and may be in the States yet, but we suspect she left the country. We will put out a nationwide alert but don't expect much action."

"This is surreal. Lindsey always did things her way, but I certainly would never have expected this. Is there anything else you need from me at this time? Should I stop in at the sheriff's office when I come up north?"

"We are good at this time, Tom. However, we will keep you informed as you are her closest relative. Thank you for the information."

Park Falls police chief Ed Collins also called in and stated that Father Hastings had not returned as of late afternoon. Housekeeper Irene Nelson had not been contacted by the priest either, leading all to believe he had left for good. Also, Agent Macklin had explained the situation to the field office who told him they could offer remote support if needed, but given the circumstances, the FBI needed to move on to more urgent matters after issuing an APB on each person. Bosworth, Macklin, and Allen gathered the evidence of the day before putting the finishing touches on a closing statement as Connie Moore called a final press conference for 7:00 p.m. Paul Handelman was contacted as well and invited to attend.

All the major media outlets in the area had a representative at the press conference.

Sheriff Bosworth began, "Ladies and gentlemen, once again thank you for showing up on short notice and cooperating with our efforts. We want to keep you informed as we have gathered a lot of solid evidence over the last few days. Eight days ago, on Sunday, the Handelman sisters were kidnapped. The kidnapping was followed by a robbery of Father Hastings' residence on Monday night. As you know, we apprehended two suspects, John Harwell and Carl Hanson, who were each charged with two counts of felony kidnapping. After considering their options, they have elected to plead no contest and provided a confession of the events. Judge Hawkins will take into account all factors in his sentencing next month, but we will avoid a trial in the case of these two.

"Rita and Theresa Handelman have returned home and are doing well by all accounts. Now this is where it gets a little crazy, so take good notes. About two weeks ago, Rita and Theresa Handelman gifted $4 million in cash to Father James Hastings to be used by the St. Joseph's Catholic Parish. This money was stolen during the robbery at Father Hastings' house last week. Harwell and Hanson have told us they were hired and that both of these crimes were orchestrated by local attorney Lindsey Barrington. Also, Father Hastings was part of this scheme. The men were given instructions to kidnap the ladies, treat them as well as possible, and release them the following Sunday. Fortunately, our hunting friend discovered them first. Also, the robbery of Father Hastings' residence was a staged event.

"The money was driven to a cabin at Butternut Lake where it was later retrieved by Barrington and Hastings who had cooked up this elaborate diversion to keep everyone occupied while skipping town. I know, I know, but trust me, this has all been backed up by evidence. Unfortunately, we did not get this confession until Sunday, which gave the two of them ample time to leave the country. The FBI is checking all flights, buses, rental cars, etc., but so far there is no sign of them. Lindsey Barrington's house was cleaned out, and she transferred a lot of her assets to her brother. Father Hastings attended a conference in Milwaukee on Thursday. He has not been seen since after telling us he would be there all weekend and would return today. Barrington and Hastings are missing.

"The FBI will release a nationwide APB for each, but there is a strong chance they are no longer on US soil. If that is the case, it will be tough if not impossible to find and prosecute them as the crime does not rise to the level of urgency needed to get our southern neighbors to cooperate fully. We will continue to collect evidence, but state and federal authorities will not be able to maintain the time commitment required. Bottom line, given the circumstances, the investigation will go into a holding pattern once evidence gathering is complete. Law enforcement will follow up on leads, but there will be no active ongoing investigation."

"That being said, this will be the last press conference at this time, and I will take questions after I give you a couple of minutes to absorb all this."

The press peppered Sheriff Bosworth with inquiries from all angles for about twenty minutes. Once it became evident that he was not going to reveal any new information, they packed up shop for the ten o'clock newscast and tomorrow's newspapers. This was an attention-grabbing story with two well-known locals at the center of it, so the news cycle promised to be very exciting.

Sheriff Bosworth walked outside and fired up a Marlboro. FBI agent Macklin joined him.

"I don't smoke, but after all this, I may start. Kind of an empty feeling."

"That's the thing with our profession, Tom, even though we had an excellent week and no one was harmed, we are still always haunted by those that got away. What could we have done better? Did we miss a lead? Same old shit every time. Never a point of satisfaction."

"This business is never easy, but I sure appreciate the way you run your operation, John. Not all counties are as organized or as professional."

Sheriff Bosworth took one more drag and stomped out his cigarette. "Thanks, Tom, right back at you. Thank you for your total cooperation with our office. We don't get that every time either."

Detective Allen walked in at this point. "Time for the mutual admiration society to break up." He laughed. "I appreciated working with both of you also. I think we should close out by stopping for a drink."

"Lead the way, and we will follow," stated Sheriff Bosworth.

Chapter 42

As Tuesday morning wound down at Ma and Pa's Bakery, Pa Chervek walked back to the kitchen to catch his breath. After last night's newscast, the morning had been record-setting as it seemed that everyone wanted to stop in for a doughnut to talk about Lindsey Barrington, Father Hastings, and rest of the players in the Handelman sisters kidnapping case. Several members of St. Joseph's Parish were among his customers.

"Can you believe Father Hastings would do such a thing? Running off with that lawyer and all that money?"

"I never trusted him. He always seemed to have other things going on."

"What do you mean? He was an excellent priest. I am still having a hard time believing he was involved. Maybe he will just be away for a couple more days."

"You will have to get over that. He is gone. Hopefully the diocese will appoint someone more stable."

And so it went among the patrons of Ma and Pa's Bakery. While some were shocked by the actions of Father Hastings, few, if any, were surprised that Lindsey Barrington was involved.

Pa grabbed a cup of coffee and took a seat next to his buddy Mike Gunther to discuss the events.

"Mike, this is unbelievable. I don't know Father Hastings, but this is not something you see every day."

"That is for sure, Pa. The whole thing is strange. Hiring two young men to do the dirty work while they take off with the spoils.

Unexpected money drives people crazy at times. Just goes to show that you never know what makes people tick."

"It doesn't surprise me with Barrington, but has Father Hastings completely lost his sense of dignity?"

"Seems that way. Some priests struggle with their chosen occupation as time moves on. Apparently, no one knew how deep his desire was to leave the priesthood."

"It sure seems odd that they would run off together as those are two opposite people."

"So we thought, but maybe they have more in common than everyone knew."

"St. Joseph's Parish and anyone associated with Attorney Barrington will have to pick up the pieces, but at least the ladies are safe."

"Amen, that's the main thing."

On Tuesday morning, Paul Handelman picked up his ringing phone.

"Hello, this is Paul."

A somewhat distraught voice on the other end replied, "Hi Paul, this is Sheila Nackers, can I please have a minute of your time?"

"Sure, Sheila, I'm pretty sure I know what you want to talk about."

"Oh, Paul, first of all, I would like to say that I had nothing to do with this. Lindsey and I are two very different people. I want to say I'm surprised by her actions, but part of me is not. I love your aunts and would advise them without collecting a fee if asked."

"I get that from my aunts. They were developing some deep distrust for Lindsey but always seemed to respect you. Also, it appears law enforcement has figured out the series of events, so I believe you."

"I don't know if you know this or not, but Lindsey and I are in the final will, so please work with Rita and Theresa to take both of us out. I don't think it is right for me to receive any money from your aunts as they have paid us well through the years."

"I did not know that, Sheila," Paul lied. "My aunts are well aware of the developments from yesterday, and I am certain that they will remove Lindsey from the will, but I think they would like to hear it straight from you. I am going over there this afternoon, so if you want to take some time out this morning to call Rita, that would be great."

"I will call her, Paul. I just feel terrible about the events that took place."

"Thank you, Sheila."

Sheila Nackers promptly placed a call to Rita stating she did not think she should be in the will and would offer her services for free going forward. Rita was a little confused as she still respected Sheila but said she would talk it over with Paul in the afternoon.

Paul pulled into Handelman Hill around 1:00 p.m. Theresa was sleeping in the front room, so he gave Aunt Rita a big hug and kiss.

"Oh, Pauly, this money is evil! Look at all the trouble it has caused."

"Well, it is gone now along with two people that you had put your trust in. Who would have known this would happen?"

"After Lindsey went crazy a couple of weeks ago and started searching the basement, we should have known better. I certainly didn't think Father Hastings would be involved though."

"I didn't either, although I had feelings of distrust for the priest that I could not rationalize at the time. Gut instinct doesn't lie most of the time."

"Sheila Nackers called and said she wanted us to remove her from our will. We had Lindsey and Sheila as primary recipients with some money going to you, Paul. We will have to redo this."

Paul acted surprised. "Yes, you will have to get Lindsey out for sure. I know a lawyer in town that can write it up the way you want. Please give it some thought and let me know before you execute. Now that Lindsey is out of the picture, you will need some help with your affairs, and I can guide you along."

"That is fine, Paul. I know I can trust you. I'm not sure if I can trust anyone else right now."

"I see Theresa is sleeping again, Aunt Rita. Is it also time we think about making some adjustments to her care?"

"Yes, we will need to do something soon. I would prefer staying here and getting some in-home care. We are to the point where someone should stay overnight to make sure Theresa doesn't wander."

"I will talk to Jen and Lisa to see if they could maybe expand their hours. Also, I'll ask if they know anyone that could join them. Those are two ladies that you should consider in your will. They love you like family and treat you wonderfully."

"I agree with everything you said, Paul. Thank you for stopping by and taking care of us."

Chapter 43

Two months later...

P uerto Vallarta, Mexico, was treating Marie Lopez wonderfully. A home had been purchased about a quarter mile off the bay with a million-dollar view. Each day, the trade winds would blow in the early afternoon to temper the heat from the constant sunshine. Rain was very rare and almost welcome when it did materialize. Marie's tennis game had improved significantly as a member of the Puerto Vallarta Sporting Club. Each morning her thoughts of the weather back home would bring a smile to her face as the two climates could not be more polar opposite this time of the year. Other than the weather, few moments were spent thinking of anything else from her past life. Generally, Marie was happy although it still bothered her that she couldn't go back to the United States.

George Hernandez, on the other hand, had been very busy. The first couple of weeks were spent doing some fishing in Zihuatanejo with local charter fishermen where he was able to land a huge tuna and several sailfish. George absolutely loved his new life, but he began to worry a little bit about being caught. He realized it had been totally foolish to kidnap the ladies as he would always be on the run for a crime that he had been a part of. Also, he did not trust Marie Lopez, so the best thing to do in his mind was to repeat his disappearing act.

George contacted Julio again through the Banco Azteca representative, and for another $40,000, Daniel Martinez was able to settle in Huatulco, Mexico, which was another area on the west coast with great fishing, a laid-back attitude, and a mix of locals with tourists. Daniel purchased a home and resumed his life as a Mexican citizen. Just like Father James Hastings, George Hernandez of Zihuatanejo ceased to exist.

Back in Price County, Carl Hanson and John Harwell had pleaded no contest to kidnapping and were each sentenced to five years of hard time. Judge Hawkins could have charged them with aiding and abetting as they held back the information, but part of him felt a little sympathy as these two men were conned into a plot that was a lot larger than they thought. Also, the victims were treated respectfully and not harmed. On the other hand, if the judge ever received the opportunity to sentence Barrington or Hastings, it would not be pretty.

As Sheriff Bosworth had predicted, most of the fallout involved family, friends, and parish members. St. Joseph's had a rotating priest for the time being until a more permanent arrangement could be found. High-ranking members of the diocese held several meetings with the parish members to help them create a roadmap to move on without Father Hastings as this situation was new to them also. As time marched on, most everyone accepted the fact that he had left the parish with the money and moved on.

Attorney Barrington's records had been seized, and her law office was shut down, causing Josie Waters to lose her job. Assistant DA Danny Jackson was in disbelief for quite some time but still recalled the morning he dropped Lindsey off at her car, so he wasn't completely shocked. Other lawyers in the area picked up Lindsey's backlog, and eventually one of them hired Josie as a paralegal.

Up at Handelman Hill, Theresa was entering the final stages of her Alzheimer's disease and was receiving around-the-clock care from Lisa, Jen, and two other excellent caregivers that had joined the home care team. Theresa could not recall anyone's name and asked the same questions over and over. It was a very sad situation, but Rita and Paul were dealing with it the best they could. As Theresa was very healthy physically, this could go on for a while. While Theresa was still of sound mind, the will was addressed. Paul is now the primary recipient of the proceeds. Others in the will include caregivers Lisa and Jen, Paul's sister and family, and finally, Sheila Nackers would be receiving a set amount. Rita and Theresa did not give any money to charity after the episode with Father Hastings.

Law enforcement had wrapped up all the investigative work, and there were no solid sightings on the APB that was listed indicating Barrington and Hastings had fled the country. The FBI didn't even bother contacting Mexican authorities as the crime did not rise to the point where they would investigate. For all intents and purposes, the case was closed, which had Sheriff Bosworth once again considering retirement. Life was moving on for most residents of Price County as the story of the Handelman sisters kidnapping was fading.

Chapter 44

While the Wisconsin winters are long and arduous at times, they do always give way to spring and eventually summer. Activity in northern Wisconsin increases dramatically during June, July, and August as residents and visitors alike know the window for warm weather is small. With the numerous waterways in the state, boating and fishing are two hugely popular undertakings.

On Fourth of July weekend, Butternut Lake was one of the many lakes in the area that featured a pontoon boat "parade," which was an excellent way to enjoy the beautiful weather. The parade consisted of pontoon boats, most decorated in red, white, and blue, joining in a line to cruise around the entire lake shore. Passengers on the pontoon boats would wave and say "Hello" or "Happy Fourth" to those on their docks or shore, who would return the greeting. Unofficial fireworks would then follow from just about every location around the lake.

Josie Waters had joined a group of her friends on a pontoon for this festivity. While circling Butternut Lake, she glanced at the people on the dock of Tom Barrington's cottage. Josie did not recognize Tom, whom she had met before, but there was a man with a very dark tan and a woman with blonde hair and sunglasses in the background. Once past the cabin a bit, she glanced back with a pair of binoculars just as the woman was removing her sunglasses. The binoculars just about dropped into the water as Josie realized this was Lindsey Barrington in disguise. She had been drinking a bit and decided to remain quiet about it on the boat but was damned sure it was Lindsey. When the pontoon reached shore again, Josie stated she was not feeling too well and drove back home.

Josie made a cup of coffee and contemplated the situation. She was still pissed off at the way Lindsey had left, leaving her with nothing except pieces to pick up. Thankfully, another job had materialized. Given it was Fourth of July weekend, she did not want to call 911 as it was not an emergency, so she dialed the sheriff's office.

"Sheriff Bosworth, how can I help you?"

"Oh, Sheriff, I'm so glad you picked up. This is Josie Waters. I used to work for Lindsey Barrington."

"Yes, I remember, what can I do for you, Ms. Waters."

"I was on a pontoon boat ride this evening with friends on Butternut Lake. As we drove by Tom Barrington's cottage, I took a little closer look just out of curiosity. A woman with short blonde hair removed her sunglasses just as I looked back with binoculars. I am sure it was Lindsey Barrington."

The frustration of the kidnapping case came flooding back to Sheriff Bosworth.

"Are you positive it was her? I didn't think she would ever come near here again."

"I am positive, either that or a dead ringer. What are you going to do, Sheriff?"

"First of all, I am going to make a few phone calls. If everything checks out, we will pay a visit."

"Thank you, please keep me posted."

"We will do that, Josie. Please keep this quiet for now. Thank you!"

The first call Sheriff Bosworth made was to Tom Barrington, who stated he did not come up to his cabin Fourth of July weekend as it was too busy. The second call was to Deputy Campbell, who returned to the sheriff's office.

"I received a call from Josie Waters stating that Lindsey Barrington was spotted at her brother's cottage on Butternut Lake."

"Seriously? What do you propose? It is already 10:00 p.m. Should we wait until the morning?"

"No, we need to go now as I want to make sure she doesn't get away again, and there is no way I would sleep tonight waiting for morning."

"All right, let's go then, the two of us should be able to cover the area."

"I'm not sure, call Roberts and have him report over. He was involved in this also so would probably enjoy bringing it to closure."

About 11:30 p.m., the three officers arrived at Butternut Lake. There were a lot of campfires and fireworks going yet, providing some cover to the two police vehicles, which came in without the lights flashing. None of this activity was going on at the Barrington cottage although the lights were on inside and there looked to be people in the kitchen. Deputies Campbell and Roberts watched the two secondary entrances while Sheriff Bosworth took the honors and entered through the unlocked front door.

"Everybody freeze! This is the Price County Sheriff's Department!"

All heeded the command except for a woman with short blonde hair who fled to the lakeside entrance. She was promptly tackled and handcuffed by Deputy Roberts.

Sheriff Bosworth took one look at the defiant eyes and knew this was Lindsey Barrington.

"Ms. Barrington, you are under arrest for the kidnapping of Rita and Theresa Handelman."

Lindsey knew the game was up and said nothing. Among the folks at the cottage was another Mexican citizen from Puerto Vallarta, Roberto Gomez. When interviewed, Roberto knew nothing of the crime, and he received an option to fly back to Mexico immediately, or he would be subject to State Department interrogation if he elected to stay in the States. Mr. Gomez boarded the next flight back to Mexico.

Judge Hawkins again wanted to avoid a trial as he didn't think it would be beneficial to anyone to revisit the events at this time and offered up less than a life sentence with a no-contest plea. Lindsey loosened up and talked to investigators once she absorbed this. Her story matched that of John Harwell and Carl Hanson.

"Why did you set up a diversion? Why didn't you just leave?"

"We figured it would occupy the police and we would be well on our way, and it worked."

"What about Carl and John? Their lives have dramatically changed although they will be in jail for less time than you."

"They knew what they were getting into."

"Why did you come back and why to your brother's cottage? That takes a lot of nerve."

"You didn't catch me the first time, I figured as a Mexican citizen I could visit without anyone knowing. We were just here for a few days."

The investigators were astounded by the arrogance. It probably took that level of self-confidence to pull off the move to Mexico. But to come back to the States? That was over the top.

Lindsey continued, "There is one more man to bring back, and I can tell you where he is for some more leniency. George Hernandez, a.k.a. Father James Hastings, now resides in Zihuatanejo. He should be easy to find once you look at real estate records."

The next day, authorities informed Lindsey that George Hernandez was not located in Zihuatanejo or anywhere near. She broke out laughing when told this information.

"What's so funny."

"I would bet that George Hernandez probably changed his name again and moved elsewhere. I have nothing more to offer on him."

Lindsey Barrington pled no-contest and received a thirty-year sentence, ending the Handelman sisters kidnapping case.

Chapter 45

On a warm mid-July evening, Paul and Jill Handelman stopped into Tony's Bar for some beer and conversation to take a break from the action of the last couple of weeks. Tony brought over two mugs of Miller Lite and a big bear hug for each of them.

"How much more do you folks have to go through? This is crazy stuff."

Paul replied, "It's unbelievable. I don't even know what to say. How could you pretend to know what Lindsey Barrington was thinking? To plan and get away with the crime takes an awful large ego, but to have the audacity to visit the region again as a Mexican citizen? Gives a whole new definition to arrogance."

Tony asked, "How are Rita and Theresa?"

Jill responded, "Rita was pretty shaken up by these events but is doing all right. Rita and Theresa may have had a lot of money, but those are some tough ladies. They have seen it all."

Paul added, "Theresa is not remembering much of anything and seems to be slipping a little physically too, so I'm not sure where that is all going to end up, but they have plenty of help. Jill and I are also over there more often. It's a relief to have everything behind us now unless Father Hastings decides to show up and conduct mass at St. Joseph's." All three laughed at this.

Tony replied, "Hastings is too smart, you won't see him again around here. I guess those rumors I was hearing and your suspicions were correct, Paul. That is something that doesn't happen every day. A priest fleeing to Mexico and leaving his parish behind. It must have been quite a struggle for him through the years."

"I don't think most people noticed," replied Paul, "but his inner conflict was visible if you looked hard enough and talked to him. Living the dream on the Handelman money."

Another hardy laugh was enjoyed by all.

"Let's change the subject." Jill smiled. "How are the Badgers looking this fall, Tony?"

Tony took off on a half hour prognostication on how the Wisconsin Badgers would be one of the top college football programs in the country. Bucky pride still burned brightly in the old offensive lineman, and it was very refreshing to see the barroom conversations finally shift back in this direction.

About the Author

J eff Rotter was born and raised in the small town of Oconto Falls, Wisconsin where he experienced many memorable times with family and friends. He currently resides in Green Bay with his family and enjoys all aspects of living in the upper Midwest.

CPSIA information can be obtained
at www.ICGtesting.com
Printed in the USA
BVHW07s1313180718
521948BV00024B/22/P